"I love this book! It shares the story of high school students whose friendship stands the test of time as they face difficult challenges. The strong bond of friendship is shown through Sophie's strength, Alice's loyalty, and Juan's bravery."

"Writers hold up before us a picture of the world. The best stories invite us into their world and ask if we recognize ourselves in it. In Alice's tale, readers will recognize themselves in her self-doubt and find themselves in her struggle to believe she has something to say. As Alice finds her voice, so does her reader."

"Alice Jarvis helps readers overcome the real and present dangers we face every day. Young and old alike will recognize the world of Closeville High School, where students meet academic setbacks, devastating diagnoses, and disappointing role models. Navigating addiction, natural disaster, and family dysfunction, this is ultimately a story about friendship and what it takes to forge your path and find your voice. The question is: Are we prepared when we know it will cost us to use it?"

"… An unflinching look at the challenge to find our footing in the world … A story of friendship and faith, setback and success, accomplishment and addiction, disaster, accusations, transitions, loss, and heartache. Through it all, the biggest challenge Alice faces is finding her own voice, and using it when it really counts."

Connect with the Author

http://on.fb.me/1HHkUXf
https://www.goodreads.com/author/show/6525216.Merrill_J_Davies
https://merrillblogs.blogspot.com/
https://www.merrilldavies.com/
https://twitter.com/MERRILLDAVIES
http://amazon.com/author/merrilljdavies
Merrill@merrilldavies.com

THE BEST
Version
of *Alice*

Merrill J. Davies

Other Novels by Merrill J. Davies

Becoming Jestina (2018)

Our Pebble in the Pond (2016)

The Truth about Katie (2013)

The Welsh Harp (2012)

© 2022

Published in the United States by Nurturing Faith Inc., Macon GA,
www.nurturingfaith.net.

Library of Congress Cataloging-in-Publication Data is available.

978-1-63528-183-5

Cover and interior design by Amy C. Cook.

Cover images:
Photo of woman by Christian Gertenback on Unsplash.
Photo of school hallway by 김은규 from Pixabay.

Dedication

This story is dedicated to the memory of Fernando Guzman.
Although his life was short, he was an inspiration to
the students, school staff, and parents who knew him.
His optimism, courage, and bravery provided
encouragement to all those around him.

Acknowledgments

I can't begin to list all those who helped me to make this novel a reality. However, there are always a few people who go out of their way to help. In this case there are three who were especially helpful.

Lila Culberson put me in touch with a large number of people to interview. These interviewees added to my understanding in such a way that I was able to create scenes that I could never have done without them.

I also want to thank Candy Brewer and my granddaughter Wyn Dempsey, who went out of their way to provide information that was helpful in describing some of the scenes in the story.

I sincerely appreciate everyone who took time to talk to me in any way.

"I think we all have blocks between us and the best version of ourselves, whether it's shyness, insecurity, anxiety, ... a physical block, and the story of a person overcoming that block to be their best self is truly inspiring because I think all of us are engaged in that every day."

—Tom Hooper, Film Director

CHAPTER 1

It is the Wednesday afternoon before our tournament, and I go by Mama's classroom to pick up my debate materials. I'm already nervous about the weekend. Mama's room is about halfway down the long hall leading to the cafeteria. As I approach her door, I hear voices. Mama is sitting behind her desk talking to one of her students as he perches atop a student desk. Apparently, he has challenged the grade she has given him on a paper. Mama looks at me wearily and tells me that she'll see me at home in a while. Grabbing my folders for debate, I trip over a forgotten backpack as I head for the door. The floor is littered with paper, signaling that Mama has not yet done her usual clean up before the janitor comes. I quietly retrieve what I need and then leave.

The parking lot is nearly empty as I get in my car to drive the few miles home. Glancing over at the pile of folders holding my debate materials about carbon emissions, I'm not sure I even understand the topic. I imagine how much work I have to do before the first round of debate on Friday afternoon. My stomach is in a knot, and my hands are shaking by the time I get inside the house. Grabbing a Diet Coke from the refrigerator, I head upstairs to my room. I decide to call Juan. He is always able to calm me down a bit.

"Hey, my friend," he answers on the first ring. "What's up?"

"I just went by Mama's room and picked up my debate stuff. I'm home now. I'm absolutely a nervous wreck."

"I assume you're worried about the debate tournament."

"Yes, of course."

"So, what exactly are you worried about?"

"For one thing, I don't even understand some of this stuff about carbon emissions. I will look so stupid, especially when they start asking me questions."

"Ah, you won't look stupid. You'll do fine. You have a great advantage: your mama's the coach. Just think about me. No one in my family even knows what a debate is."

"Having Mama as the coach doesn't help. It makes it worse for me because everyone expects me to do well."

"Who is 'everyone'?"

"You know, everyone."

"When you think about it, Alice, it's probably just me, or maybe some members of our debate team. The people you're debating don't expect any more of you."

"You don't know."

"Yes, I'm pretty sure."

I can see Juan grinning, probably shifting in "Betty," as he calls his wheelchair, or on his living room sofa.

"Why?"

"Because most of the kids you're debating don't even know your mother's a coach."

I think for a moment. "Oh, I guess not," I concede.

"See? You have nothing to worry about."

"Did you know that Clifton High School is probably several times the size of Closeville?"

"What does the size of the school where the tournament is held have to do with anything? ... Wait, hold that thought. I've got to get a Coke."

Juan always helps me see how ridiculous some of my fears are—not that it helps much, but at least I can laugh at myself a little. When I think of our friendship over the years, I can't believe that I rely on him for support as much or more than he relies on me.

I met Juan the summer before I started 7th grade. My friends and I had walked over to watch some kids play soccer. This boy whizzed right by us so close, I could have touched him. Someone yelled, "Hey Juan!" He was dark-skinned, skinny, and fast! I asked who he was.

"Oh, that's Juan Garcia," my friend said. "He's new and will be in 7th grade, just like we are." She went on to explain that he had several younger brothers. His mother came from Mexico, but all the kids were born in the U.S. My friend thought they moved to Georgia from Texas. We watched them play soccer most days the rest of the summer.

That fall, Juan was in my English class and we became good friends. He taught me a lot about soccer. Sometimes I helped him with English, but Juan was good at most everything. He didn't need much help. The way I remember him in 7th grade was that he was always running—playing soccer, football, basketball, or jogging down the sidewalk after school.

Sometime during that year, he learned that he had osteosarcoma, and had to have his leg amputated during the summer. My dad, who is a physician, says osteosarcoma is a type of bone cancer that is most common in children and young adults. It often spreads to the lungs or other parts of the body. Juan's cancer left him unable to play sports and run. For a while he snapped at me for every little thing I did wrong, and he wouldn't talk to me as much.

Suddenly I am jerked back into the present by a rustling, and Juan says, "Okay. I'm back."

"Are you and Bert ready for the tournament?" I ask, shuffling through my papers to find one of my briefs.

"Not really. We started to work on it, but then I found out I wouldn't be going."

"Why not?"

"Because I have a doctor's appointment Friday in Atlanta."

"Oh, I'm sorry. You should have told me. Is something wrong?"

"Oh, no. It's just a check-up, or report or something. My doctor at St. Jude's has been in contact with my doctors in Atlanta about the tests I had there a few weeks ago. But you know, when I have to go down there it basically takes all day."

"Is Rosa taking you?"

"No, she has to work, but she called the school, and Ms. Willoughby said she'd take me."

"Well, be sure to text me when you get home."

"Oh, I will. Look, you will do fine this weekend. You're a good debater. You just have to believe in yourself."

"But how do I do that? I see you and Sophie and the others, and all of you seem to know how to present your case. When I get up there, I see the judges looking at me. I feel so unsure, especially during the crossfire. I can't tell if they're sorry for me, or if they just think I'm dumb."

"Well, when I first lost my leg in 7th grade, I felt very self-conscious. I thought everyone was just looking at my leg… The thing is, other people can't see the way we feel. When I see you up there giving a speech or answering questions, you look fine and seem to know what you're talking about. Just remember that. Go on out there and give it a try. Eventually, maybe you'll forget about what others are thinking."

"Okay. I'll try. I guess I need to get off the phone. I see Mama coming in the driveway. Be sure to text me when you get home Friday."

When I end the phone call, I'm not so uptight about the tournament. I feel badly that I have dumped all my problems on Juan, but it's always been like that. Juan never makes me feel like he's the one who has a problem. And he can sometimes be a little crass with me. I have never let him get away with much, though.

Once when Mama dropped me off at the hospital to stay with Juan a while, she came in for a moment. She was just leaving, and before she got out of sight, Juan looked at me and said, "Who dressed you today? You look awful!"

I jumped up and looked out the door. "Well, I'll just leave then! Mom!" I yelled. She turned around, but before I could say anything, Juan apologized. He's like that. He will sometimes say really ugly things, but he usually apologizes. I think that's the way he reacts when he's worried or sad.

After his leg was amputated, it took him several months to get back to being like the friend we all knew. Eventually though, he became very determined to make the best of his life—a fighter, a "warrior," he said. Now he goes to all the soccer games to support his friends. He's their biggest fan.

Over the last few years, the osteosarcoma has spread to Juan's lungs and he has had several surgeries, including the amputation of an arm. At some point during that time, Juan started living with his godparents. He never said why. He just said he'd moved in with them, and I didn't ask any questions. Even though he's been through a lot, Juan is the one I always go to when I am upset. He seldom mentions his own problems unless I ask. I can't believe we will be seniors this fall.

I want to be strong, like Juan and my other friends. I want to be the one who encourages my friends and doesn't complain. But first I have to get through the debate tournament this weekend. I'm just sorry Juan and Bert aren't going with us this time.

Chapter 2

What's wrong with you? You're white as a sheet!" says Sophie as I walk up to her. She is sitting in the Clifton High School cafeteria beside Jason and Todd, our debate partners.

"Nothin'," I mutter. I look around the huge cafeteria at the two or three hundred people gathered to begin the last tournament of the season. It doesn't calm my nerves.

"You threw up again, didn't you?" Sophie's dark eyes looked straight into mine.

I nod. I always throw up just before the pairings come out for the first round in these tournaments. I've tried all the little tricks people have suggested: Take deep breaths. Imagine the audience in their underwear. Imagine yourself feeling confident and winning a trophy. But I still get sick every time.

"Why do you get so nervous? It's just a debate—although this one is special! Do you realize we'll be seniors after this season?" Sophie grins at me, her dark curls framing her round face.

"I know." I have not been quite as nervous giving constructive speeches this year, but I still hate the crossfire part when I face difficult questions.

"Alice, you really need to get over being so shy. What if you really needed to speak up for someone, a friend maybe—like me, or Todd?"

I shrug my shoulders.

"Seriously," Sophie presses. "I mean, what if one of us were in trouble? You'd just stand there and say nothing, wouldn't you? You wouldn't have the guts to stand up for us!"

I feel the blush in my cheeks, wishing she'd lower her voice. She may be right. I don't know if I could. At Closeville High we're almost like family, so we're expected to help one another.

"You'll do fine today, Alice," Todd says softly as he looks our way. "I think you're doing much better during crossfire than you did at the beginning of the year."

Todd's blue eyes seem sympathetic to my plight, and that's encouraging. If I can just make it through this season, there'll be a summer break before another one comes around. When I got in 9th grade, Mama thought being on her debate team would help me overcome my shyness. I thought so too, at the time. Now I'm wondering if I've really made progress. I want to think I am gaining confidence, but sometimes I wonder.

"Where's Juan and Bert?" asks Jason, Sophie's debate partner. "Why didn't they come with us?"

Before I can answer, Sophie speaks up. "Juan had a doctor's appointment."

I remember that Juan said he'd text me when he got home. Juan is really my best friend, but most of my friends don't understand about having a boy as your best friend, so I usually say Sophie is my best friend—and she is in a way.

Sophie is very outgoing. She'll talk to anyone. Juan once said, "Sophie would talk to a fence post." I think that's a saying he heard from his godmother Rosa, but it describes Sophie perfectly. One time we went to a Chick-fil-A and there was a statue of Truett Cathy, the founder, sitting on a bench in front of the building, and I swear she sat right down beside him and started talking to him!

Both Juan and Sophie joined the debate team when we were in the 10th grade. Sophie missed school a lot, but I learned quickly that she was no dummy. She can outthink me most of the time, and she can outtalk me all the time!

I listen as Sophie, Jason, and Todd continue to talk, but my mind wanders. I am back in 3rd grade, attending a birthday party for my friend Cheryl. I'm standing in her living room with some red-looking drink pouring down my light blue dress onto the off-white carpet, and everyone is laughing. I watch in horror as Cheryl's mother enters.

Suddenly I realize Sophie is talking to me.

"Alice, where do you want to go to college?"

Sophie always says the only way she'll be able to attend college is to get a good scholarship. I have no clue where I'll attend college, but I know I'll go.

"I don't know."

"I might get a basketball scholarship. Maybe Coach Callahan can help me."

Sophie is on the Closeville girls' basketball team. They won the region tournament and will be going on to the state playoffs. Their big win has made superstars of them this week. Their coach teaches history just two doors down from my mother, so I see him almost every day but haven't had him for a class. Everyone seems to like him though.

Todd adds, "If anyone can help you, Coach Callahan can."

"You really think so?" asks Sophie.

"Yeah. He's a good history teacher. Most of the textbooks skim over things that students want to know more about, especially topics such as the Japanese internment during World War II and the Trail of Tears. Coach Callahan answers our questions and tells us where we can get more information."

"Well, I don't know anything about that," says Sophie. "I just know he's a good coach."

"I like delving into all sorts of issues in history. That's why I like debate so much."

I could see that Sophie didn't want to talk about Todd's interest in history. She soon turns to me.

"Alice, can you believe we won that basketball game last night? I thought for sure the other team would win, but Coach Callahan said that we could win, and we did! He is the best coach ever!"

"Yeah, I heard your team did great. I'm sorry I couldn't go."

As usual, I wanted to say more, to explain, to apologize. Dad had bought tickets to a concert weeks before I knew our girls' team would be in the region playoffs.

Todd speaks up, just as excited about the game as he was about discussing history and debate. "I was there. It was awesome! Our team was down five points when I went to the concession stand and up by two when I returned!"

Todd is on the boys' basketball team, and they did well too, but didn't win region. I'm glad Mama made us partners on the debate team. Todd is such a good team player and never makes me feel bad when I goof up. I think he's that way on the basketball team too. He's only about 5 feet-10 inches tall, but he's a good solid player. He doesn't try to be the star, just a valuable member of the team. He doesn't get stressed out about anything. If I had to describe Todd with one word, it would be "solid." I can always count on him—for help, for encouragement, to do the right thing, not to get upset. I guess some people would say that's boring, but I'm okay with boring.

Sophie is beaming. "I was so excited when I got home, I couldn't sleep. My mom said it was the first time in 20 years that CHS had won region. She said it was all because of Coach Callahan."

"Did your mom make it to the game?" I ask.

"No, of course not. She had to work late. Dad promised to come, but he didn't make it either." Sophie's face was expressionless. I think she is unhappy when she talks about her mom and dad.

Jason says apologetically, "I'm sorry I didn't make it, Sophie. Somebody has to make sure we're ready for the debate tournament, you know."

He grinned, his dark eyes shining. Jason never goes to any of the sports events. He says it's a waste of time. He was kidding her about having to stay home, but it is difficult when we have debate tournaments and basketball tournaments the same week.

"Look," he says, a bunch of papers dangling from his long, skinny arm. "I practically rewrote our whole case on the Pro side. I practiced reading it to my family."

I can't imagine Todd doing that, but Jason's father is a history professor at Kennesaw State University, so maybe their family would actually sit and listen to the reading of a debate brief.

"Thank you! It needed a lot of work," says Sophie.

Jason and Sophie are alike in some ways. They want to win at everything. I'm not sure they really work as a team, but they win a lot more trophies than Todd and I do. Jason is very smart. Mama sometimes says he's "too smart for his own good." I'm not sure what she means by that, but I think it has to do with his ability to communicate with average people. He's not shy like I am, though. He talks a lot. He just says off-the-wall things and often offends people. Sometimes I wish I could be like that. Anyway, he is a good debater, but I'm glad he's not my partner.

Mom is judging the first round today, so as soon as the pairings are announced, she rushes off to her room, telling us to meet back in here after our round is finished. She has to judge most of the time. Coaches have to provide a judge based on how many teams they bring, and since our school doesn't provide much financial help to the debate team, Mom usually judges rather than pay for one. I'm not sure how it works. I just know that she has to judge most of the time.

Todd and I draw Clifton in the first round. That's bad, because they can usually beat us easily. To make matters worse, we lose in the coin toss and Clifton makes us go first. Todd and I think our case for adopting a carbon tax looks pretty good, so we choose to debate Pro in this round.

We always start out the same way, so today I begin my Constructive speech: "Resolved, that the U.S. government should adopt a carbon tax."

I look around and see the Clifton senior rustling through his notes.

I continue: "We acknowledge that there is a need for designing the carbon tax in a way that channels at least some of the revenues to low-income households through a portfolio of existing social safety-net programs."

Boring stuff, I know, but I continue through my first brief.

"In British Columbia, Canada, the main proceeds of carbon pricing go directly to firms' households—making the carbon tax quite popular among important political constituencies. A global carbon tax may be a problem for some parts of the world, especially in underdeveloped countries. There may be a need for a carbon tax to reflect different abilities to pay. As a plan for protecting the environment, though, it's a good idea."

When I finish, Todd gives me a thumbs up. I feel pretty good until Clifton's first Constructive speaker gets up and quotes almost all of a paragraph in my speech.

He looks at the judge and says, "The source my opponent used here was debunked six months after it was published."

As my confidence sinks, he goes on to give other sources that directly contradict mine. When he finishes, Todd takes as much prep time as he can. I try to help by pointing out a few things in the brief that might help. Todd rebuilds our case the best he can, focusing on our best sources.

Clifton's second speaker doesn't do quite as well as their first, but I still dread the rebuttals, not quite sure how to refute Todd's initial arguments against one of my sources. I basically try to argue that our other sources outweigh that one.

Crossfires never go well for me, but I try. I actually challenge my opponent.

"You obviously haven't read the study by…."

In the end, I feel like I have defended my position against some of my opponent's assertions. Even so, both Todd and I are so rattled by the time we present our final two-minute speeches that Todd mouths, "We're dead!" I agree.

Finally, we finish the round and walk slowly back to the cafeteria, discussing the problems we had in the round. We have been there about a minute when Mama walks in.

"How did it go?" she asks, looking from one of us to the other.

"Oh, Mrs. Jarvis, they killed us," Todd replies.

"Maybe it wasn't as bad as you thought."

I appreciate her effort to comfort us, but I am not convinced.

"Oh, yes, it was. I got off to a bad start, and we could never get back any momentum." I know our failure is my fault.

Todd says reassuringly, "But Alice, you had a good crossfire. She really stood up to that guy, Mrs. Jarvis."

I look at Todd, glad that he noticed my improvement. I am determined.

"You'll do better in the next round," Mama said.

"Let's hope," says Todd. "Here come Sophie and Jason. I bet they won, as usual. I'll go ahead and call that round!"

"How'd it go?" Mama asks.

"They didn't stand a chance," Jason answers.

Sophie shakes her head, indicating that he may be too confident. Jason is always sure they've won, but Sophie is a little more realistic.

We all laugh, and then Sophie and I rush off to the bathroom before the next round. We barely get back to the cafeteria and sit down at a table when we hear an announcement over the loud speaker.

"May I have your attention? We have pairings ready for round two. Listen carefully: Closeville A vs Carrollton B in Room C103, Clifton C vs Closeville B in Room D201..."

As the speaker announces each team and the room number, we begin to gather our materials and exit the cafeteria.

Todd and I are the "A" team, so we head to C103, which is a long way from the cafeteria. This time we win the coin toss and we speak second, countering the resolution with our arguments. I actually think the carbon tax is a good idea, but in debate that doesn't matter. What matters is that we know both sides and can state them in a convincing way.

Carrollton states the arguments for a carbon tax in much the same way we do in our case, with a few exceptions. Their argument, like ours, says that those who cause environmental harms should be made to pay the full social cost of their actions.

"I have some good evidence from my hometown that a higher tax on carbon emissions can discourage investment and economic growth," I begin.

I pull out my article from the Closeville newspaper and read where some company refused to come to our town because of a certain tax on carbon emissions.

"Any tax like this can discourage industry from investing in our towns. Also, a tax on carbon emissions often encourages firms that pollute to hide their actions and therefore avoid paying."

I drone on and on about how difficult it is to measure the external cost and how much tax to charge and the costs of administrating such a tax.

"In addition to these disadvantages, it forces firms to shift their production to countries that don't have a carbon tax." I cite two cases where this is true.

"In conclusion, a carbon tax can only work if there are economic and viable alternatives that people can choose and use. Many large cities in the U.S. have poor public transportation. Stop driving cars and use what to get across the city?"

I feel fairly confident when I sit down, an unusual feeling for me.

Carrollton uses the same example we did about British Colombia's success with the carbon tax, and we are ready because we have had to counter the same argument in our debate with Clifton.

"Australia tried the carbon tax and it lasted about two years," begins Todd, when he is up to speak.

The crossfire is intense, but both Todd and I think we are able to hold our own.

Finally, the tournament is over, and we return to the cafeteria for the awards ceremony. My mind goes in all different directions when the tournament director begins speaking. I'm wondering why I still haven't heard from Juan. I think about the homework I have to do when I get home. Suddenly, I hear my name being called out from the platform. What? Is he still announcing awards, or are we being called out for something we've done wrong? Sophie is elbowing me and smiling. Todd stands, and grabs me by the arm.

"Come on, Alice," he says.

When we reach the platform, Todd lets me in front of him to accept the shiny trophy. It is engraved with the name of the tournament and the date, and the division of the Georgia High School Association we are in. The teams in these tournaments are divided just like the sports teams are, according to location and size.

For the first time I feel that I have made a little progress. It's about time! Maybe I'll do even better next year.

I'm glad the tournament is over, and we get in the van to go home. After they all congratulate us, things get quiet in the van.

I'm a little worried because I haven't heard anything from Juan. Last spring, he broke his left arm. Then during the summer, he went back to the doctor for a check-up and the next thing I knew they told me he'd had his arm amputated. I made Mama take me to see him in the hospital in Atlanta. I was scared for Juan, but he just said, "When they told me there was tissue around the metal rod that had cancer in it, I just told them to cut it off!" I guess when you've had cancer for as long as Juan has, you aren't as scared as I would be. Or maybe he's just learned to cover up his fear.

Sophie and Todd are rattling on about the basketball tournament. I'm happy for Sophie, but I can't think of anything to add. I'm glad Todd plays basketball too, because he knows how she feels. I'm not into sports that much, so I often don't know what they're talking about. Jason is even worse than I am, so it's up to Todd to talk basketball with Sophie.

"Our coach is good, but not as good as Coach Callahan," Todd comments. "I have watched Callahan, and he's really good."

Todd and Jason begin talking about their upcoming history test, and Sophie and I are talking about the tournament. Sophie always does better than I do, but she never makes me feel bad. Soon she starts talking about basketball again. I tune her out and think about a paper I have to write for American Literature.

"Alice, did you hear me?" Sophie asks.

"I'm sorry. No, I didn't."

"I asked you if you want to go with me to Callahan's Monday night," she says. "A bunch of us go over there on Mondays, and I thought you might like to go too."

"Do I know anyone who'll be there?"

"Well, you know me, and you know Todd, and Juan usually comes too."

"I guess I can go if it's okay with Mama."

"If what's okay with me?" Mama asks from the front seat of the van.

"Can I go with Sophie to Callahan's Monday after school?"

"Sure, if you can get your homework done."

I promise that I'll take care of my homework first.

I'm glad Todd and Juan will be at Coach Callahan's house. Juan has been my friend for a long time, of course. Todd joined the debate team the same year I did as a freshman. We have never been close friends, but we work well together. I think Mama knew that he would be a "safe" person to be my debate partner because he is so easy going. I think that most of the others might be critical when I make mistakes or freeze up when I am expected to talk.

Todd must have heard our conversation about coming to the coach's house on Monday night.

"So, I guess I'll see you girls Monday night," he says when we drop him off at school.

I watch him as he walks to his car. It's an old blue, beat-up-looking one—a Ford, I think. His steps are measured, and he looks confident. I wonder what it's like at his home. He doesn't say much about his family, but I know he lives on a small farm several miles from town.

CHAPTER 3

I t turns out that Sophie's car is in the shop. I think about this as I pull into her driveway. A part of me can't help but wonder if that is why she invited me to come to Callahan's house in the first place—to be her ride.

"Thanks for picking me up," Sophie says as she gets in my car, looking all fresh and cute.

"You look like you've changed clothes since school."

"Yes. I went home, showered, and changed. Mondays are long and grueling. We have basketball practice right after school, so I have no time in between."

Coach Callahan lives just outside Closeville on several acres of land. Closeville is a small city of 35,000–40,000 people in Northwest Georgia. It's not along the interstate, so as Dad said the other day, "It's not on the way to anywhere." It's a pretty town, and considered a safe place with a good "family atmosphere"—whatever that means. The coach's place looks like it's out in the country, but it only takes about 15 minutes to get there from Sophie's.

I hope Juan will be there because I still haven't heard from him about his doctor's appointment. Sometimes he rides with me places, but of course he wouldn't know I am going to Coach Callahan's tonight. I should have called him. He's about the only one I ever call: I just dread calling people. I always imagine that when they see my name come up on their caller ID they don't really want to answer.

We get to Callahan's about 7:30, and there are already a few cars in the driveway. It's a typical three-bedroom, ranch-style home with rolling hills in the background. I'm a little nervous, but I try to stay calm. The coach comes to the door and gives us a hug. He is a bigger man than he seems at school. He isn't too tall, but he is heavier than I realized. Maybe it's because he is wearing a UGA T-shirt and blue jeans. At school he usually looks a little more dressed up with his shirt tucked in and a sports jacket.

"It's about time you got here," he says to Sophie. "It's good you could come too, Alice."

As we walk in and shed our jackets here and there, Todd enters the living room with a Coke can in one hand and a small dessert plate stacked with assorted cookies and chips in the other.

"I'm glad you came, Alice," he says. "I haven't seen you since—Saturday!"

I laugh. It makes me a little more comfortable to have him here because I don't know most of the others.

Todd is accompanied by a guy that I've seen around school, but don't know personally. He is taller than Todd.

"Alice, Joe here is a junior on the basketball team. Joe, do you know Alice?"

I hate to be the center of attention, but I smile and try to be friendly.

"Not really," Joe responds. "I just know she's Mrs. Jarvis' daughter, which probably means she's real smart."

I never can decide if it's an advantage to be the daughter of a teacher or not. In one sense it is, because most of the kids like Mama. But it's embarrassing too.

"Of course, she's smart. She's my debate partner," says Todd affirmingly.

I am blushing at the compliment, but I can't think of anything appropriate to say, so I stay quiet and continue to smile. It means a lot to hear Todd say that I'm smart. At least it gives his friend a positive view of me.

Joe and Todd begin talking about some movie they saw, and I walk into the kitchen.

Several people are standing around munching on cookies, chips, nuts, and other snacks.

Sophie asks, "Alice, do you know Grace?"

A blond girl with beautiful, shoulder-length curls is standing there with a bottle of water in her hand.

"Not exactly, but I think I've heard Juan talk about her."

I turn to Grace and say, "You and Juan go to church together, right?"

In our school, most of the kids attend some church. I don't think it's like that everywhere, but in small Georgia towns like ours, the church is often an important part of one's social life. I am a little surprised that Juan goes to the same church as Grace, though. Juan's family is Catholic, and the church Grace goes to is Baptist. That doesn't happen real often. I'll ask him why when I talk to him.

"As a matter of fact, we do," Grace confirms.

We talk a little and I learn that she plans to be a nurse. I wonder why I have not seen her around school more. After we talk a while, I realize that we did have a class together as freshmen, but she looks different now. I sense that she is a very kind person. She seems especially at ease around all of us. I ask her if she has heard from Juan since his doctor's visit on Friday. She says she hasn't.

I have never met Mrs. Callahan, so I am looking around for her. When I ask where she is, Grace says she works out of town and will be here later. I think that is strange. I can't imagine my dad having anyone, especially teenagers, over when Mama isn't home. There are three other girls here who are on the girls' basketball team, and all of them talk a lot to Coach Callahan about the winning game last week. I just listen. All the girls are excited about winning, and he keeps referring to things that happened in an "inside joke" kind of way. Something about this situation makes me uncomfortable. The coach doesn't say much to me, and I'm glad he doesn't. I keep watching for Juan, thinking he might drive up at some point. Usually when he comes by himself to an event where we all are, some of us go out and help him out of his car.

Mrs. Callahan finally gets home around 9 o'clock. When she enters, things get quiet for a moment and then everyone goes on talking. I know immediately who she is, although I don't remember seeing her before. She is tall and thin and is wearing a burgundy-colored jacket over her beige-colored sweater and black slacks. She looks very professional, like the receptionist at my dad's office. She goes to a closet and hangs up her jacket. She looks tired, and at first I think she isn't happy about us being there. She is nice to us, though, and when Sophie introduces me, Mrs. Callahan asks us about our debate tournament this past weekend.

"I work for an optometrist close to Clifton High School," she tells us.

After speaking to some of the other people, she goes into the kitchen.

Coach Callahan is showing the boys a new play he's working on for the girls' team. I notice how different he and Mrs. Callahan seem. A few of the girls go into the kitchen and get some more cookies. Not long after that, Sophie says we'd better head home.

On the way home, Sophie chats about what everyone said. She obviously had a wonderful time. Sometimes I wish I was less anxious in crowds so I could enjoy things as Sophie does.

"I can't believe Coach Callahan would have kids over after school like that," I interject, "especially since his wife was late getting home. My dad would never have anyone over when Mama isn't there."

"Well, Coach Callahan likes for us to come over. He's such a good coach. Closeville has never had a really good girls' team before. You wouldn't believe how hard he works to help us win. We all have certain things to work on, and he keeps reminding us of what we need to do. He doesn't criticize us when we make a mistake, though; he just encourages us to do better next time."

Sophie is all excited about her basketball team and keeps referring to things they discussed during the evening and explaining some of the things she knew I had not understood. I don't say anything, and I wonder why I didn't enjoy the evening like Sophie did.

When I get home, I can't get the evening out of my mind. On the one hand, maybe I am just uncomfortable around people with an outgoing personality because I'm afraid I'll look stupid to Sophie. For some reason I don't like Coach Callahan, and I didn't enjoy being at his house. I don't understand why Sophie would rather spend time at her coach's house than her own. She has never asked me to come over to her house and spend the night, or even just to come over in the evening. I think she may be afraid to. I really don't know. And Todd is the same way. He never talks about where he lives. I don't often invite people over either, but I have had a group from our class over for my birthday parties and sometimes around Christmas or Valentine's Day. With all these thoughts of Callahan, Sophie, and Juan whirling around in my mind, I have trouble falling asleep. Finally, an idea enters my mind and I fall asleep.

The next morning during breakfast I ask, "Could we have the debate team over on Monday evenings to hang out, and maybe talk about debate a little? It doesn't have to be an official practice. You all don't even have to do anything. I'll fix some snacks, and we can listen to music or something."

Mama pulls out her phone and looks at her calendar. Dad looks as if I've asked him to entertain aliens in our house.

Finally, Dad sighs. "I guess so. Prue, are you going to be here? What time will they come?"

"Maybe 7:00 or 7:30?"

"I think that would work," says Mama. "But we'll have to eat before then. I guess we can do that."

"As long as you'll be here, it's okay with me," says Dad, looking at Mama.

Dad is very smart, but he's not too good in a crowd—especially a crowd of teenagers.

"Of course. I wouldn't leave you here alone with a bunch of teenagers," Mama says, laughing.

She is comfortable having my friends around. She knows most of them, and she knows all the debate team of course. Dad has met all of the team, but he seems awkward with kids in general.

I am not surprised that Mama agreed for the team to come over on Mondays, but I wasn't sure about Dad. He is quiet—like I am—so I never know what he'll say. He's not exactly unpredictable. It's just that he likes his routine. Maybe it's his scientific mind. Everything has to be in order. Although I am quiet and shy as he is, I am not a scientific person. I'm more artistic. Anyway, I'm relieved that both my parents are okay with the team coming over on Mondays. Sophie and Juan will be at our house instead of Coach Callahan's. I like that idea. I can't wait to tell Sophie. I just hope she'll want to come.

CHAPTER 4

On Tuesday at school, I don't see Juan. I begin to worry. I ask Sophie if she has seen him. She hasn't either. Although I have known Juan for much longer than Sophie has, the two of them have more in common. One day not long after Sophie met Juan, she said she had to go home early from a soccer game to take care of her little sister.

Juan said, "Oh, I know all about that. I have five younger brothers. I worry about them all the time."

Sophie looked surprised. "Really? I didn't know that. Sometimes I feel like the mother of my little sister."

Juan laughed. "Well, I don't feel like the mother, but I've always had to look after my little brothers a lot. One of these days I'll be a doctor and they'll have everything they need."

After having that conversation, Juan and Sophie have often compared notes about helping with their siblings. Juan can always identify with whatever our problems are, despite having much bigger issues to deal with than we do. He just never talks about them much.

Sophie only has one little sister to help with and Juan has five brothers, but he acts like her problem is just as great as his. I wish I could be as helpful to him as he is to me. I don't even have a sibling to worry about, and even if I did, my parents would be the ones caring for both of us. Sometimes it makes me ashamed to express my fears of talking to people. But when I tell him I'm afraid to do something, he acts like it's important and tries to help me find a way to cope. That's just Juan.

When I was in 10th grade our English teacher assigned a speech as a major portion of our grade during the first grading period. I was terrified, sure I would make a bad grade and embarrass Mama. The first person I told, of course, was Juan. He listened carefully to my fears.

"Okay, you can do this. First of all, you write speeches for debate all the time," he said.

"I know, but this is different. In debate I just read the research and things that others have said. This is a personal speech about something I've done."

"You've done things," he reminded me. "You've gone on trips with your family, you took an art class last summer, you've sat with friends in the hospital," he said with a wink and a smile.

By the time we finished talking, I felt better, thinking that maybe I could to it. And I did! It was during that time that I realized how much I enjoyed writing.

When I get home from school, I look at my phone to see if Juan has sent me a text, but he hasn't. Fed up with not knowing what is going on with him, I send him a text asking if I can come over.

After about five minutes, my phone buzzes and I look at his answer: "Sure." I grab my car keys and tell Mama I'm going over to Juan's. As I drive over there, I have a scary feeling that the doctor's report might not have been good. I hope I am wrong.

I knock on the door, but don't hear anything at first. Then I hear Juan's voice. "Coming."

He opens the door and motions for me to come in.

"Are you okay?" he asks as soon as I'm inside. "I hope nothing's wrong."

"I'm fine. I thought you would text me Friday when you got back from the doctor."

"I'm sorry. I got busy and forgot that I was supposed to let you know about the doctor's visit," he says. "Carlos called and said Leon was sick, so we went over there, and I just forgot. I ended up staying with them yesterday and part of today." (Carlos and Leon are Juan's younger brothers.)

"So, what did the doctor say?" I ask, though not sure I want to know.

"Well, the news was not good. You know, I told you that I made a quick decision to let them amputate my arm last summer? Well, I did that because I hoped the cancer wouldn't come back. But the doctor says it has."

"What will they do this time?"

Juan sits there for a bit, as if trying to decide what to tell me.

"Nothing they can do, the doctor says. They give me three to six months."

Before I can answer, he smiles and continues: "But they don't know Juan Garcia. I will walk across that stage and graduate from high school, and the 'big C' can't stop me!"

Caught up in his optimism, all I can say is "Of course, you will walk across the stage."

He nods his head and grins. "Hey, let's go to the soccer field and watch practice."

"Okay. You ready?"

"I will be in a second," he answers, as he pushes himself back into Betty (his wheelchair—I can't remember why he started calling it that).

In a short time, we are on our way to the soccer field. At first, I can't think of anything except his bad news. But he just acts like usual, talking about the soccer players and other unimportant things.

While we're driving, I tell him that Mama wants the debate team to come to our house on Mondays. I make it sound like it was her idea.

"We don't have to actually work on our cases all the time, though. We'll just hang out, and we can talk about debate if we want to. I know you usually go to Coach Callahan's on Mondays. I hope that's not a problem."

"No, it won't be—at least not for me. I'll tell Bert. I'm sure he can come. I love your mama. She's helped me a lot lately. You may have to come get me next week, though, because I've got to have work done on my car."

"I can do that."

My mind keeps spinning. Three to six months? Who will I talk to when I'm upset? I know I shouldn't be worried about myself, but I am.

We pull into the practice field parking, and I help Juan get out of the car and into his wheelchair. When we reach the bleachers, some of the team members come over and give Juan a high five, and he greets them with his usual mischievous grin. It all seems so surreal. Juan is acting as if nothing is wrong.

I see Sophie's car pull onto the field, and I want to run and tell her about Juan's bad news, but I don't; it's not my place to tell her.

As Sophie walks up, she waves to some of the players, most of whom are already on the field, and then approaches Juan.

"Why were you absent from school today and yesterday?"

"I had to do some stuff with my brothers. I'll be there tomorrow."

"How did your doctor's visit go last week? I haven't talked to you since then."

Juan shifts slightly in his chair before answering. "Uh, it was okay… What happened at the coach's Monday night? I had to catch up on school work from Friday, so I didn't go."

"It was fun. Guess who came with me?"

Juan shrugs.

"Didn't she tell you?" asks Sophie. "Alice came with me."

"Really? Alice, are you trying to hide things?" Juan says in laughter.

Then Sophie comes to where I am sitting and I tell her about my Monday night plans.

"Sophie, I know you usually go to Coach Callahan's on Mondays, but Mama says she'd like for the debate team to come to our house on Mondays this spring, just to hang out and get ready for our last tournament. Could you come?"

"Sure. Have you asked the others?"

"I asked Juan, and he said he'd tell Bert."

Sophie likes the idea and says she'll tell Jason and Todd. They all like Mama because she is easygoing. Unlike the sports teams, which are always getting in the school news, the debate team never gets much attention. Most people at CHS don't even know what debate is. I wish they knew how much work goes into putting together a case and getting ready for a tournament.

When Juan and I leave the soccer field, I ask him, "Why didn't you tell Sophie what the doctor said?"

"Because, like I told you, the doctor doesn't know me. I will graduate from high school next spring."

"But aren't you going to tell anyone what the doctor said? Even though I believe you, I can't just ignore his prognosis." I can't imagine not telling anyone, but I hate to tell our friends if Juan doesn't want it told.

"I just don't want everyone to go around all long-faced all the time because they think I'm going to die soon, because I'm not."

"I understand. It's just that it's hard not to tell some people, especially Sophie."

"If you want to tell Sophie and some of the others what he said, I don't care. I guess I'll have to tell a few people. Just be sure to tell them I'm not giving up. I'll be around for graduation."

"I know. I'll tell them not to be talking about it all the time," I promise.

But when I take him home and head to my house, it's all I can think about.

As soon as I get home, I tell Mama what Juan's doctor said. I can tell she is upset.

"How is Juan handling it?" she asks.

I tell her what he has said and then question her. "Do you think I should call Sophie and tell her? I just don't know what is right. I want to help him deal with it, but I'm afraid I'll make it worse."

Mama is quiet for a bit before answering. "Maybe it will be easier for him if his friends hear it from you. At least he has given you permission to tell people."

"I thought about that. It might be that he's sort of asking me to tell our friends. Anyway, I think I'll go upstairs and call Sophie."

"Just remember," Mama reminded me. "I'm always here for you and your friends. I know this is a hard time for all of you."

"Thanks."

In our phone conversation, after our usual banter about school stuff and debate, I change the subject.

"Sophie, I called to tell you I talked to Juan after school today."

"And.... Is he all right?" she asks.

"Well, no—not really. His doctor has given him three to six months to live."

The line goes silent for what seems like a whole minute or longer.

"Sophie?"

When she responds, her voice is shaking a little.

"Are you sure? What...why...I mean he said nothing about it to me this afternoon."

"I know. He had told me before we came to the practice field, so I asked him why he didn't tell you, and he just said he didn't want everyone to be 'long faced' or something like that. But he did say I could tell you."

I tell Sophie what Juan said about being around for graduation. Then she and I alternate between talking and crying for an hour or so.

The next morning at school I tell Todd about Juan's doctor's visit. I think Sophie tells Jason and Juan tells Bert. Anyway, word gets around, but I think we all honor Juan's desire for life to go on as usual, without being "long faced" or talking about his situation when we are around him.

Through the spring months I watch for signs that Juan is getting worse, but he is always upbeat and never complains. He is the most positive person in our group.

When I tell him that I met his friend Grace, who goes to his church, he says, "Actually, I go to her church. She was already there and invited me to go with her."

"I thought you were Catholic. Why did you start going to her church?"

"We were talking about God and our beliefs one day at school, and she asked if I'd like to go with her. My godparents don't go to our church much because they work most days, so I agreed to go with Grace, and I like her church. They have a lot of stuff for people our age."

I don't know much about that church. I go to one closer to where we live. I'm glad that Juan likes going to Grace's church, though.

"How do you stay so positive with all you've been through the last few years?" I ask.

He answers immediately. "My faith."

"Exactly what do you mean by that?"

I've heard all the sermons about faith, and I'm a believer, but I'm having trouble imagining how it would feel to be told I have three to six months to live. Juan's faith must be stronger than mine.

"Well, I believe there is a God and that he loves me." He stops for a moment to think. "If I live a long time, I want to help a lot of other people who have problems. If I don't live long, then I need to stay busy getting as much done as I can."

Juan does just that. He always encourages folks in our group to be happy. Sometimes when one of us complains about some little frustration we have, he'll look down at himself and say, "Look at me. If I can smile, you can smile."

As I think about Juan and his faith, I am reminded of our community and school and how we work together to help one another. I'm not sure why Juan lives with his godparents instead of his mother, but he has several "mamas" at CHS and in our community. They have taken him to cancer treatments, stayed with him in the hospital, and let him hang out in their homes when his godparents needed them. Our town's not perfect, but we all depend on one another a lot. I hope that I can do my part.

CHAPTER 5

One of Juan's "mamas" is Martha Lucas. She is our beautician, and her daughter Isabella has been my friend since 9th grade. We haven't spent as much time together as we used to before Sophie and I became friends, but we still get together some. Isabella is probably the smartest girl in our class. I'm pretty sure she will be the valedictorian. When I first met her, she said she wanted to be a doctor. One time she spent the night at my house and picked my dad's brain about oral surgery all evening instead of taking part in our typical sleepover activities. I thought it was interesting that Dad was talking to one of my friends so much that night.

Isabella and her mother have helped get Juan to many of his treatments and stayed with him in the hospital multiple times. Now Isabella is interested in the research side of medicine because of Juan.

Just before school is out for the summer, Isabella calls me one afternoon as I'm pulling into my driveway. "Alice, has your mother told you about Juan's trip to California?"

"No. What trip?"

"It's a long story. After you told me about what the doctor said about Juan, I told Mom. One day when he was at our house, Mom asked him if he could do anything or go anywhere, where would he like to go. He first said he wanted to see Dwayne 'the Rock' Johnson, and then he said he would like to go see the *Ellen DeGeneres Show* in person."

"Are you saying he is going to the *Ellen DeGeneres Show?*"

"Well, after Mom asked him that, she and some other people contacted the producers of the show and they were interested. One of the concerns they have had all along is that Juan might not be able to go if they put it off too long. Now all of a sudden, they were asked to come in just a few days."

"Is he going by himself, or is his family going with him?" I ask.

"None of Juan's family can go with him, and he doesn't want to go to California alone," Isabella replies.

"Who is going then?"

"Mom is willing to go with him, but they need someone from the staff at CHS to go also, since he'll be out of school for a few days."

"So, who did she ask? Or, has she asked anyone yet?"

I'm thinking about whether she might ask my mother, but I doubt that. She probably asked Ms. Willoughby, the counselor.

"That's why I asked if you'd heard about the trip. She was planning to ask your mother, but I haven't talked to Mom yet. I just thought if Mom had talked to your mother, you might know."

"No, I haven't talked to my mom either."

"The other reason I called was to suggest that you and I talk them into taking us along."

"Do you think they'd actually do that?"

"I don't know. Although Juan might not say so, you know he needs some friends to go with him."

"For sure, he won't want to go with two adults—especially women."

"It's all settled, then. We'll both try to convince our mothers to let us go too—provided that your mother is willing to go."

As soon as Mom comes home, she tells me about the trip, and I begin my plea to take Isabella and me along. Mom's main objection is the cost. The *Ellen DeGeneres Show* is paying for Juan's basic expenses and for Mrs. Lucas' plane ticket and hotel room.

Mom and Ms. Lucas talk back and forth a couple of times about taking Isabella and me along.

Finally, they decide to pay for us to go. I think my argument that Juan won't have much fun going with two adults wins Mom over. Juan is always fun to be around. He makes me think that I can be somebody someday. Juan says I might be a great writer, a "best-selling author."

A lot of the parents, teachers, students, and others in the community have contributed money through a GoFundMe account so that Juan can do the things he wants to do. Several parents and teachers give Mom and Mrs. Lucas extra funds so Juan will have spending money, and everyone wants him to be able to shop for some souvenirs too.

We are scheduled for an early flight to California on Saturday morning. I can't get to sleep. Mom said I needed to go to bed early, and I did, but I am wide awake. I keep thinking of things I need to pack, or what I will need to do in the morning. I get a text from Isabella, then I text her back. She is having the same problem. Finally, sometime after midnight, I succumb to sleep. Suddenly, Mom is shaking me and telling me it's time to get up.

At the airport there is lots of help for Juan, which he hates because it attracts so much attention; and he likes to just blend in with the crowd. This is awful. He can easily get to his own seat on the plane, but they strap him in this weird little armless chair and take him to his seat. When we finally get to Los Angeles, the flight attendants say they'll have someone come to his seat to get him. Finally, Juan stands up and holds on to the seats as he hops and jumps along to the front and says, "Bring me my wheelchair." He is not in a terribly good mood by the time we get to the rental car. We all get in and head for our hotel.

Since we're not going to the TV show until Tuesday, we have Sunday and Monday to sightsee and shop. On Sunday we go to Venice Beach and Huntington Beach and enjoy the best ice cream sundae with churros! We spend a lot of time people-watching.

On Monday we visit Santa Monica. We shop some in the morning. At the Converse place they let Juan design his own shoe, and he puts the word "survivor" on it. Of course, he only has one foot, so Isabella and I remind him that half the pair is useless. He doesn't care. He loves shoes, so he bought shoes in several different places. Going down the street, Mom is pushing his wheelchair, Isabella and I are carrying all the shoes in bags, and Ms. Lucas is carrying the rest of Juan's purchases. We make an unusual scene as we parade down the street.

After we put all Juan's purchases in the car, he gets the idea to ride the roller coaster and the ferris wheel overlooking the Pacific Ocean. I decide not to ride with him, but Isabella does. I've never been much for those kinds of rides, but Juan loves it. Later we go to a place called Back to the Beach Café, where we literally sit with our feet in the sand while we eat.

We go to Malibu that night and eat at Duke's, another restaurant right on the beach. On the way back Juan starts to sing "Bless the Lord, Oh My Soul," and Isabella and I join in. We are singing at the top of our lungs. I can see the lights ahead from the Santa Monica pier. I look over at Mom, and I think I see tears in her eyes. I don't know whether they are tears of happiness or sadness, but I keep singing. I guess we are all wondering if this will be the last time Juan will take a trip with us.

When we get back to the hotel, Isabella and I start packing our things because it is our last night there. Our room is right next door to our mom's, and Juan's room is just across the hall.

That night Isabella tells me a little more about osteosarcoma. She hopes that one day she will be one of the medical scientists to find a cure. She is applying to Case Western Reserve University, where she says only about a third of the students are accepted each year. This school is known for having the first program for medical scientists.

"I wish I had been in college 10 years ago," says Isabella. "I might could have come up with a cure for Juan."

During the trip we haven't talked any about Juan's illness. We're just pretending the trip is for some other reason. Juan doesn't want to talk about it, so we don't.

Tuesday is our big day—the day Juan is to visit the *Ellen DeGeneres Show*. He won't actually be on the show, but he gets to be in the audience. I am so amazed at how much Juan is able to do for himself. I had never really thought about it before. He has only one hand and yet he manages to get his clothes on, tie his pants off at the missing leg, and tie his shoe.

The people at the *Ellen DeGeneres Show* send a driver to our hotel to pick us up. We check out and the driver takes us to the Warner Brothers studios. When we finally get there, we go in through the back lot. Our driver points out Ellen's Porsche sitting in the parking lot. When we enter, we are directed to a dressing room with Juan's name on it.

He keeps saying, "This doesn't seem real. This is crazy."

There's room for only two guests, so Ms. Lucas and Juan enter through a side door and are squeezed in right in front of the stage. Isabella, Mom, and I have to stay backstage. They bring in a chair for Ms. Lucas, and Juan sits in his wheelchair. We can hear everything, but we can't be in the audience. There is a very small area where we can peek through and see where Juan and Ms. Lucas are sitting, but only one of us can look through it at a time. Ellen goes down into the audience and dances with Juan briefly, and during one of the commercials, she has a picture taken with him. After the show, the driver who brought us from the hotel picks us up and takes us to the airport. Juan is quiet.

"Did you enjoy the show?" I ask.

"It was fantastic. I can't believe I actually sat there and then had my picture made with Ellen. I'm sorry you, your mother, and Isabella couldn't be in there though."

"We could see you through the curtain," says Isabella. "It was just like being there."

"What all are we missing in schoolwork for Monday and Tuesday?" asks Juan.

"I haven't a clue," I respond.

Isabella, always the scholar, adds, "I did my math and history Friday night, and I talked my English teacher into letting me do a speech about the trip to make up for that assignment."

"Teacher's pet," accuses Juan.

"It'll be some work, but it won't be too difficult," says Isabella.

"I can't believe you would volunteer to do a speech. I would never do that."

"I know, but for me it will be easy. I'd rather do that than turn in a paper."

I can't believe a speech in English class would be considered easy, but I guess for Isabella it is. Of course, for Isabella everything is easy.

CHAPTER 6

It's two weeks after the last day of school, and Sophie and I are in my room talking about what we've been doing since then. She's been babysitting with her little sister most of the time, and I haven't done much except browse the Internet and write a few poems.

Summer is my favorite time of the year, not because of the weather, and not exactly because school is out—although that is part of it. I love summers because I don't feel any pressure to interact with other people. I enjoy being by myself and not having to "perform" for anyone—no speeches in class, no debates, no meeting new people. I can just relax and spend a little time with close friends—and write. This summer I have signed up for an online class in writing fiction, mostly short stories.

"You're going to do what?" asks Sophie when I tell her of my plans.

"I'm going to take a course in writing fiction. It's a class I read about online. It's a six-week course and you can submit parts of the story and professional writers will give feedback. At the end of the course, you can submit your story to different contests if you want to."

"Does it cost a lot to take the course?"

"Not really. I think it's $100 or something like that, but it's not too much. I got some money for my birthday that I can use, and Dad says he'll pay for the rest. I haven't actually signed up yet, but I'm going to."

Sophie looks at me like I've grown two heads. "If you want to, I guess that's okay."

As usual, I feel a little bad because Sophie doesn't understand my interest in writing. Then I realize that I don't understand why she spends so much time with basketball. I realize that just because we're different doesn't mean we can't be friends. Usually, when Sophie and I have a conversation like this, I leave feeling if I'm wrong or something.

"It makes no sense to you that I would spend time during the summer studying writing, does it?" I comment.

"No, it doesn't," she says, laughing.

"Well, it doesn't make much sense to me that you spend so much time practicing basketball either. But you like it, and that's okay." I smile at her and she smiles back. "So, it's okay that I want to learn to write better, even though you don't understand it."

"Now that you put it that way, I guess you're right. Why do you think we're so different and yet we can be friends?"

"I was thinking about that the other day. I read an article about introverts and extroverts in this magazine. I had always thought it was just about being shy or outgoing, but that is not quite right."

"Really? So, what is it about then?"

The article said that it has to do with what energizes us. Some of us are energized by being around other people, and others are energized by being alone."

"So, what does that have to do with us?"

"Well, if I understand it right, you probably are an extrovert. You are energized by being around a lot of people, which makes you enjoy going to parties and playing basketball. But I'm probably an introvert. I would just as soon stay home—and write!"

"Well, that explains a lot. When I go to a game or a party, I usually feel great when I get home."

"And I'm tired and need to go to my room and read."

"It also explains why we both enjoy just talking—like this—so let's go to the DQ and get some ice cream."

While driving to the Dairy Queen I say to Sophie, "You said something a few months ago that I've thought a lot about. You said that I needed to overcome my shyness because I might need to 'stand up for a friend, like you or Todd'."

"Yes, and…?"

"How do I do that? I just get embarrassed and scared when I have to talk to people that I don't know well. I feel so stupid."

"You're not stupid, that's for sure. In fact, I was just thinking you might tutor me a little this summer in English."

"Why?"

"Well, my grades are not that good, especially in English, and I really need to get my GPA up before I start applying to colleges. I think that if I can get really good grades this fall it will help a little."

"Of course, I'll be glad to help if I can. Why do you think your grades are low in English? What do we need to work on?"

"Probably a lot of things, but the main thing is that every time I got a low grade on a paper last year, the teacher said something about organization. I always think I'm improving, but apparently, I'm not. Do you think you could help me understand what I'm doing wrong?"

"I think I can. I'll see if Mom has some materials we can use to practice."

"That would be great. One of my problems is that I was absent from school a lot in the 9th and 10th grades because I always had to help with my little sister. I missed out on a lot of the basics they taught."

"Yeah, I think they do a lot with learning to organize things in 9th grade, but you'll catch on fast."

Later that day, I realize that Sophie values me and my abilities even if I am lacking in some ways, just as I value her although she is weak in some areas. It gives me some confidence that maybe I can do more than I thought. I feel stronger somehow, and share with Mom what Sophie and I have discussed.

"Sophie wants me to coach her in English this summer. She wants to get better grades in writing. Do you have any worksheets or practice exercises that would help her in organizing her thoughts?"

"Probably. Do you need my help?"

"No. I just wanted to look for some ideas to start with."

I am amazed at myself. In the past, I would have just let her do it. But this time I want to do it by myself.

Mom points toward her desk in the corner of the den. "There is a folder in the top drawer that is labeled 'Writing.' See what you can find there."

I look through the materials and end up taking the folder upstairs with me. Soon I have a plan for helping Sophie learn how to organize her ideas better. I call her and we come up with a schedule where she will come to my house every Wednesday and I will work with her for a couple of hours.

When I tell Mom about my plan, she laughs and says, "You may decide to be an English teacher!"

"I don't think so. I just hope I can help Sophie bring her GPA up a little."

"Well, I am proud of you for being willing to help her."

During our first tutoring session I have Sophie write a paper "free style" so I can see how she does without help. I have listed several topics for her to choose from, making sure to have at least one relating to basketball. Of course, she chooses that one. When I read the paper, I understand what her English teacher is talking about. Her ideas are jumbled up—not organized in a way the reader can make sense of them easily.

I look forward to the sessions with Sophie. I plan to give her one idea each week about how to organize what she writes.

At our second session, I have her rewrite the basketball paper. Since she decides to write about the region championship, I suggest that she approach it from a chronological perspective. Then, I offer up some transitional phrases that will help her sentences flow better.

In the next few weeks, I have Sophie write a paper one week and revise it the next by using various organizational methods. By the end of our sessions, she feels confident enough to delve into senior English. She seems proud of her accomplishments, and I feel good about having helped her.

Other than helping Sophie, I spend most of my time on my online fiction writing course. I love learning all about plot, setting, and character development. It's not an interactive course, except that I can submit what I write each time through email and someone evaluates it. I can do my work any time of day or night. Most of the time my feedback is positive, with a few suggestions.

At the end of my online course, I have the opportunity to submit one of my stories to a contest, but it's not required. I look through the contest options and choose a national contest that I think fits the kind of stories I write. The deadline is not until September 1, so I'll have time to revise my story. When I reread all six of the stories I have written, I immediately cull out four of them. The other two could use some revision, but I can't decide which one I want to revise. One of them is science fiction. The other is more realistic and contemporary. I print a copy of both of the stories and go downstairs where Mom is looking at a brochure about river cruises.

"Are we going on a cruise?" I ask.

"Probably not. I'm just looking," she answers.

"Well, do you want to see some of the stories I've written this summer?"

"Yes, I certainly do. Have you finished the course?"

"Yes. I wrote several stories, but I brought two that I wanted you to read and tell me which one you like the best."

"What will you do with them?"

"Oh, probably nothing. I don't know. I just want to get your reaction."

I hand the printed stories to her and head for the kitchen for a Diet Coke and a piece of fudge. When I come back through the den, Mom is still reading the stories, so I go back upstairs and check my email.

Before I can finish going through my emails, Mom bursts into my room and says, "Wow! These are both good!"

"You really like them?"

"Yes! I had a hard time deciding which I like best. I think I like the futuristic one, though, just because it's so creative. You should consider sending one or both of them to a magazine or something, have them published. I'll be glad to help you do that."

I start to tell her that I already have a plan to submit one of the stories to a contest, but I don't.

"I might do that. I think I'll just do a little more work on them first."

As the summer draws to a close, I begin to dread the new school year. In one sense I have gained confidence over the summer, but that confidence does not seem to be carrying over into the beginning of school. The dread I always feel at this time of year is still pervasive the week before school starts.

CHAPTER 7

I can't believe it's my senior year in high school. All these years I've thought it was such a big thing. I thought it would never get here, but here it is. I don't feel any different. In fact, I'm kind of scared. I thought by this time I wouldn't be so afraid to speak out, but I still am. My goal this year is to learn to communicate better. I do fairly well when I'm reading a debate brief, but I still hate to cross-examine the opponents, and I hate to be cross-examined even more. As silly as it sounds, I've been using my free time over the summer to practice my talking.

Last week, when I took Sophie home to get her debate material before we went to practice, I tried to talk to her dad while she went into her room. Mr. Bargo kept asking me what we were doing in debate, but I didn't explain it very well. He listened to me talk about what we were debating a little, and then he said, "You mean kids will be able to lock stuff up in their lockers and the staff can't get into it? What if they have drugs or guns in there?" I'm glad Sophie walked out of her room about that time, because I didn't think that conversation was going to turn out well. At least I tried.

I sent my short story in to the contest just before school started, so I won't know if I win or not for several months. Simply placing in the contest would help me to believe in myself. Even if I don't win, I can at least be proud of the short story I've written all by myself. It definitely is unique. The idea came to me after a conversation with Juan about his cancer. I used this writing exercise to explore what might happen if someone from another planet had the cure for cancer. I was glad Mom liked it best, but she doesn't know I submitted it to the contest. The winner gets $1000!

We've been spending a lot of time practicing for debate the last few weeks. Our debate resolutions change every month or so. About the time I begin to get comfortable with one topic, it's time to change to the next one. The topic this fall is "Resolved, in U.S. public K–12 schools, the probable cause standard ought to apply to searches of students." That's what I was trying to explain to Sophie's dad.

Today we're heading to Chattahoochee High School. It's a big tournament and I dread it. Mom is driving the van this weekend because we're bringing all three teams. We pull into the crowded parking lot and Mom tries to find a parking space.

"Just pull in down there," says Bert, pointing down toward the end of the lot. "Todd and Jason can help me with Juan's chair, and it'll be easy."

Usually, Todd and Jason help push Juan's wheelchair, except when he and Bert go in a different direction for a debate round. Bert would push it all the time, but the guys just hang together when they are not debating.

"Yeah, and we can make Alice and Sophie help too!" says Juan.

I'm glad Juan could come. He and Bert are really good.

"Yes, Alice and Sophie get off way too easy. We went to some country in Africa once where the women did all the work, and the men just sat and watched," says Bert. His dad is an attorney who has traveled all over the world.

Bert and Juan make the weekend fun. They are both very outspoken, and they make up all these crazy debate resolutions on the way to and from tournaments just to make the rest of us laugh. Today they came up with this one: "Resolved: the school system should increase the debate coaches' supplements from $0 to something."

We find a place to park, and then Bert gets Juan's wheelchair out. He pushes the chair most of the way through the parking lot, but Todd grabs it just as they start up the ramp. Inside the building, we go down a long hall and into the auditorium where lots of students are waiting for instructions.

Our teams work together to do research and brainstorm ideas, but when it comes to writing the briefs, we divide the responsibility so that everyone has an equal amount of work. We are all comparing notes.

"Bert wrote our Pro position this time," says Juan. "But I wrote the Con. It looks pretty good, doesn't it Alice?" I nod.

"Bert, did your dad help you and Juan write these briefs?" asks Todd, looking at Bert's speech. "This sounds like lawyer talk."

"No, no, he didn't," insists Juan. "He wasn't even there. We came up with both briefs all on our own, didn't we Bert?"

"Yes, we did, thanks to old Juan Garcia, who thinks outside the box. How would you know what 'lawyer talk' sounds like anyway?" asks Bert, looking at Todd.

I keep listening to them and thinking that someone who doesn't know Juan would never guess that he might not even live to graduate.

When the pairings come out, Todd and I go against Cherokee County High School. They have a good team, and we'll be going to their tournament later in the year. When we got our topic this fall, Todd had said, "Oh, I like this. They can't just search our lockers for no good purpose if this gets adopted."

"Just remember, there are arguments for both sides," Mom reminds us.

And sure enough, when we started reading all about this topic, we realized that there are some good reasons for not adopting it. There are arguments for both sides. You have to look at all the arguments. That's one thing I've learned in debate. It's easy to just listen to what your friends think or what a political party says. In debate you can't do that.

In the coin toss we lose and have to go first, but we get to choose which side to argue, and we choose Con because we think our brief is stronger on that side. I speak first and begin by citing the *New Jersey vs. TLO* case in 1985, and end by saying that the Con position is that schools need and deserve flexibility due to their position as caregivers and educators. The flexibility aids them in keeping students safe. I go on to cite several reputable sources saying that public school students don't have unlimited rights in most areas because schools take on a sur-rogate parent role known as *in loco parentis* ("in place of parents").

I feel pretty good about our arguments, and Todd does too. Cherokee's first speaker does a good job with the Pro argument, but Todd and I find loopholes in it. He follows up with information on the role of school resource officers, and then concludes by saying that students have sufficient freedom and protection of their rights without making all searches at school follow the "probable cause" standard that adults do in formal court proceedings.

We are confident through the rebuttals, although I still hate the crossfire por-tion. I notice that one of the judges is nodding his head while Todd gives our last rebuttal speech, so that gives me hope.

When our teams get back together, all of us agree that we had a good round, and we're ready to take on the next one.

"Guess what?" Sophie asks me while we wait for the pairings.

"What?"

"I might get a basketball scholarship!"

"Really? Which college?"

"The University of Cincinnati in Ohio!"

"Cool… How did you learn about it? Have you applied?"

"Wade—Coach Callahan—told me about it. No, I haven't applied yet, but it's where he went and he said he'd recommend me."

"Oh… That's exciting."

I remember my feelings the night I visited at the coach's house, and my stom-ach tightens.

"He told me last night when we were at his house after practice."

I'm happy for Sophie, but I am surprised that she is going to Coach Callahan's again this year. I wonder why it bothers me so much, and I realize that my family hasn't been having the debate team over on Mondays this fall.

I wish I could talk to someone about my feelings about Coach Callahan. I know that everyone else likes him a lot. I think if Sophie or Juan felt the way I do about anyone, they'd just say it out loud no matter who it was. But I can't do that. I think it would be unfair to Callahan. Maybe it's because I haven't had a class with him.

After our debate rounds are over for the day, we load into the van and head out. I'm feeling a little bolder today, so I decide to bring up the subject of the coach with Sophie.

"Sophie," I ask, "do you feel comfortable around Coach Callahan?"

"Of course. Why?"

"I don't know. I just feel very uncomfortable around him sometimes."

"Alice, you're uncomfortable around everybody. You just need to grow up. You're almost pathological in your inability to talk to people. It's embarrassing sometimes."

"Okay then, maybe I am 'pathological'—whatever that means."

Sophie is probably right. Maybe what the doctor told Mom was wrong. Maybe my problem is bigger than I think. I feel bad about asking Sophie about the coach now. I don't say anything for a while.

I guess Sophie thinks she's hurt my feelings, so she looks at me and apologizes. "I'm sorry, Alice. I didn't mean to be ugly to you. It's okay—you're okay. But I don't know why you're uncomfortable around the coach. If you played basketball, you'd feel differently."

During the next break, I overhear Todd telling Jason that he's applied for a basketball scholarship. But I don't hear the details, so I ask him, "Did you say you've applied for a basketball scholarship?"

"Yes, I meant to tell you. Thank you for suggesting I talk to Ms. Willoughby. She was a lot of help. I've applied for three different scholarships, and plan to find some more."

"Great."

"My dad has heart problems, and my mom is really worried about him. I would hate to go far away from home as long as he's sick."

The day goes by fast with one round after another, with a quick lunch break squeezed in the middle.

It seems as if no time passes until the tournament is over and we are ready to head home. One-day tournaments are stressful every time, and we are always exhausted. When Juan is able to go, we all do better. He and Bert make us feel successful, even when we lose a round.

My mind keeps coming back to the fact that Juan might not always be with us. He was voted "Most School Spirit" in our senior class last week, and he gave a speech where he said, "None of us are guaranteed tomorrow, so I intend to live my life to the fullest and continue giving back to others through my experiences and my 'never give up' example." I think of those words and feel panic in my chest.

CHAPTER 8

It is Sunday afternoon when my phone buzzes. I think it may be Juan texting me, but it's Sophie.

"Is it okay if Joline and I come over for a while?"

Joline is Sophie's 5-year-old sister. I wonder why she wants to come over, but of course I type a quick "yes" and send it back. I am a little worried that something is wrong. I go downstairs and tell Mom that they are coming over. Dad is playing golf this afternoon and won't be home until late.

"Is everything okay with her?" Mom asks.

"I don't know. It worries me a little because she sounded upset."

"I'll play with Joline so you all can visit," she says.

In about 15 minutes I see Sophie pull into our driveway. When she and Joline come in, Mom immediately gets some of my old toys out of a closet. Soon Sophie is assured that Joline will be happy playing with Mom, and we head upstairs to my room.

"I'm sorry to interrupt your Sunday afternoon. I hope your mother doesn't mind."

"Oh, no. It's fine. I think Mom's enjoying having a little one to entertain... Is everything okay?"

"Not really. I haven't said much to you about it, but my dad drinks a lot."

"Oh..."

I don't want to tell Sophie that I already suspected this, but I don't want to act shocked either. She seems pretty upset.

"I just had to get Joline out of the house for a while. Dad was gone all day yesterday and all night. When he came home, Mom was furious, and they started yelling at each other. Sometimes I just wish he would leave and not come back. But at other times, I just don't know."

I want to tell Sophie that I understand, but I really don't. I have no idea what she's going through. Finally, I just say, "You're welcome to come here any time."

"Thank you. I really appreciate you and your mom," Sophie responds, with sad eyes rimmed in red and makeup streaked down her cheeks. "I can't wait to go away to college. I hope I can go to law school. Maybe I can help other kids who have problems like I'm having."

"You would make a great lawyer," I assure her.

"I hope so. Sometimes I think I just want to get away from home, so I don't have to deal with all this crap. Then I feel guilty about leaving Joline."

"You can't fix everything."

"I know. Maybe when I leave, Mom will have to do something. As long as I am home, she just lets me take care of Joline when she has to work late. Dad won't do his part."

Lying across my bed, Sophie and I talk about school and debate and basketball. Occasionally we hear Mom and Joline downstairs laughing.

Finally, getting up and pushing back her dark curls, Sophie says, "I guess I'd better rescue your mom from Joline and take her home."

"You know you are always welcome here. I think Mom is enjoying Joline."

Sophie tells me it's okay to share with Mom what she has told me about her dad, and we walk downstairs.

"Thank you so much for playing with Joline. I know she's been having fun," Sophie tells Mom. "Come on Joline, let's go home."

"But I don't want to go! We're not through, are we?" She looks at Mom.

"Of course we're not, dear, so that means you'll have to come back again so we can continue."

Joline looks troubled, but she gives in when Mom promises that she can come and play again soon.

"Joline is adorable," Mom says when they leave.

"Yes, she is. I feel sorry for her, though."

I tell Mom all that Sophie has said. We agree it is an unpleasant situation, but there is not much we can do. No one else can fix it. All we can do is support Sophie and Joline when they ask. For the first time I feel that I am an important part of the "family" at our school, and I can be part of the solution to the problems of others. I may be shy, but I have my own way of supporting my friends.

"I'm glad Sophie wants to get out of that situation and go to college. Maybe she won't end up like her mother."

"I hope she won't," says Mom. "The thing is, her mother has to stand up for herself and her kids. Lots of people have problems with alcohol and drugs, and they have to deal with them. Sophie may be right. When she leaves, her mother may be forced to make some decisions that will help Joline."

I know I am lucky to have the kind of parents I have. Sometimes I take them for granted. I often feel sorry for Sophie's parents. I don't think either of them have much education or training. Even though her mother works a lot, it doesn't seem like she makes much money.

After her impromptu visit, however, Sophie seems a little distant to me. I see her every day, but she doesn't say a lot. She seems quieter. I think maybe something is wrong, but when I ask her, she says she's fine. I wonder if she's afraid I've told people about her situation at home. I hope she knows I wouldn't do that.

CHAPTER 9

I have spent more time with Grace since I met her that day at Coach Callahan's last spring. She is not like most of my friends. She's quiet, yet radiates confidence. When we're together, we often talk about Juan. I wonder if she has picked up on my dependence on him and my fear of losing him.

On a Saturday morning when we are sitting at my dining room table eating freshly baked banana nut muffins, Grace asks, "You've known Juan for a long time, haven't you?"

"Since 7th grade."

The morning sun is shining in on Grace's golden curls and I think she looks like I imagine Goldilocks looked.

"So, you knew him before he lost his leg?"

"Yeah. I often think of him running. When I first met him, he was always running—on the soccer field, on the baseball field, on the sidewalk. He loved to run. And then…he couldn't."

I stopped, and I realized I was about to cry.

"I'm sorry. I can tell that Juan has depended on you for a long time."

"Not really. The fact is, I have depended on him. He's helped me much more than I have helped him."

"He told me that you visited and stayed with him in the hospital many times."

"I have, but… You don't know what a pitiful mess I've been—and still am."

Grace tries to reassure me. "We all have our problems. That's the reason I think having a strong faith is so important."

"I don't know. It doesn't seem like it's helping Juan much right now."

I guess I sound bitter and angry, but that's the way I feel.

"I think God will take care of him. Even if he doesn't get well, God will help him accept everything. Juan is growing in his faith."

I had not heard anyone talk like that before, so I was surprised and asked Grace, "What do you mean?"

"I just think he's learning to depend on a higher power to take care of him. He's studying the Bible, learning about God, and taking it all in. He says he knows there is a God and that his life is in God's hands, so he's not worried about his illness or about his family life anymore."

I have noticed a difference in Juan, too. He seems more at peace with himself. Until this year I have never known anyone facing death. Grace seems to have a better understanding of it all than I do.

"I'm glad Juan is going to your church, Grace. I don't know what to say that will help him."

I am feeling bad that I seem to have no wisdom to pass along to my friend.

Grace must sense that I am feeling bad about myself. She looks across the table at me, smiling, and says, "But you are always there for him. Even if you don't say anything, he knows you care."

It makes me feel so good to hear that.

CHAPTER 10

Not long before Thanksgiving break, I see a picture of a man who has been arrested for DUI. Although I don't know Sophie's dad's full name—I just always call him Mr. Bargo—I'm almost sure it's him, based on the age and address listed. I don't know whether to mention it to Sophie or not, so I don't say anything, and have forgotten about seeing it.

The time between Thanksgiving and Christmas is always rushed at my house. We start shopping as soon as Thanksgiving is over, but we stay busy right on up until Christmas.

One Saturday morning Mom comes up to my room as I'm getting out of the shower and asks, "What are your plans for the day?"

"I was thinking it would be a good day to go shopping this afternoon."

"Okay. I need to finish a few decorations this morning, but we might go sometime after lunch."

I make a list of things I want to get before I go downstairs.

Just as we finish lunch and are putting away our dishes, my phone rings. I see that it's Sophie. I almost don't answer.

"Hey, Sophie."

"Alice, do you have a minute? I need to ask a favor."

I can tell by her voice something is wrong.

"Sure."

Sounding as if she's almost in tears, she asks, "Can I come over? I really need to talk to you."

"Well…" I almost say that we are about to go shopping, but I don't. "Sure, come on over."

When she comes in, her eyes look red and I'm sure she's been crying on the way over. We go upstairs and she starts crying the minute I close my door.

"Oh, Alice, what am I going to do?"

I don't know what to say, so I ask, "Do you need anything?"

"I don't know. I'm sure you saw where my dad was arrested a few weeks ago for DUI."

I nod my head yes.

"When he got out, Mom filed for divorce. I'm glad she did in a way, but everything is getting so complicated now."

"In what way?"

"Well, they fight all the time. Mom asked him to move out, and he did. And then he came back and begged her to let him stay 'til after Christmas. She first said that he could not, and then he said that she wasn't being fair to Joline, and she gave in."

As Sophie talks, she is crying and getting louder. Some of the time I can't even understand what she is saying. I am about to cry with her. I don't know what to say. Then there is a knock on my door, and Sophie stops in mid-sentence.

"It's just Mom. Is it okay for her to come in?"

"Yes, it's okay," she says, calming down a bit.

I open the door.

Mom comes in and wraps her arms around Sophie, holding her for several moments as she sobs. "It's going to be alright, Sophie. You'll get through this. It may take a while, but you will."

"I know," Sophie says, sniffling. "But I worry about so many things."

"Let's just take things one day at a time," says Mom. "What's your biggest worry today? If you could solve one problem today, what would it be?"

"I guess it's about Joline. It's almost Christmas, and Mom doesn't have any presents for her… But there's no way to solve that today. I don't think there's money for presents this year. I can accept that, but Joline, she's…."

"Maybe we can do a little something to help with that today. What if you and Alice and I go shopping and get Joline a few things this afternoon? I love to buy for kids." Mom looks at me and smiles. "And my little girl is all grown up."

"Oh, Mrs. Jarvis, I can't let you do that!"

"Why not? You wouldn't want to deny me the privilege of getting that sweet little 5-year-old a few toys, now, would you?"

"I just feel so bad, coming and dumping all this on you," Sophie says. But she has perked up a little. She sits up straight on my bed, reaches for a tissue, and wipes her eyes.

"Come on," I urge her. "It'll be fun. Mom and I were thinking of going shopping anyway."

"Okay… if you're sure."

"We're sure," Mom and I say at the same time.

Soon we are on our way to the toy store. Mom was serious about how she misses buying little girl toys. She used to love buying for me when I was little and taking me shopping. Sophie is reluctant to suggest anything, so I pick up some things and ask her and Mom what they think. We find a doll that is popular with kids this Christmas season and some accessories for it.

Mom picks up a little tea set. "Joline was fascinated with a tea set like this that was in Alice's old toy box. Let's get it for her."

Soon we have several packages that we all agree will make Joline happy.

"Can we go home and wrap them?" I ask. They agree.

By the time Sophie and I get the presents wrapped, it is dark outside.

"Can you stay for dinner?" I ask Sophie.

"Oh, no, I'd better go home. I guess they're wondering where I've been so long. I've messed up your whole afternoon already. Should I leave these presents here for a few days or take them with me?" she asks, looking at the packages.

We all agree that she should leave them at our house until closer to Christmas, and Sophie seems a little more relaxed.

She pauses in the middle of the living room as she picks up her jacket. "I can't tell you how much I appreciate you both for letting me dump all my problems on you."

Mom and I assure her that it is okay to come to our house any time she needs to vent her feelings as she deals with the problems at her home. Sophie thanks us again and hugs both of us before she leaves.

As Sophie backs out of the driveway and Mom and I are walking toward the kitchen, she tells me, "I am really proud of you."

"Why? What did I do?"

"I'm proud that you are the kind of friend that someone like Sophie can come to when she needs a shoulder to cry on."

CHAPTER 11

The day we get out for a two-week Christmas break, Juan tells me that Grace is going to sing in the Christmas program at their church this Sunday evening. I can tell that he wants me to go, but I act like I thought of it myself.

"Can anybody come?" I ask.

"Of course," he says. "Do you want to come?"

"I'd love to. And I might bring Sophie. Is that okay?"

"Sure. The more the merrier," he says.

By Sunday afternoon I have enlisted Sophie, Jason, and Todd to come with me. When I call Juan, he seems excited. He says he'll be there when we arrive because he's helping display the lights. He and Grace are spending a lot of time together now. She even told me that his godparents have warmed up to her, too. I feel a little bit left out and jealous of this development but remember that my relationship with Juan is different. I am merely a friend. I may be wrong, but I think Juan and Grace have a different sort of relationship, although neither of them has said anything specific.

When we arrive, there are already a number of cars in the church parking lot. It's a large brick building, and Juan told us to park on the right side of the building and enter the door at the back. He said he or Grace would meet us there and show us the best place to sit. I send him a text when we get close to the church to let him know we are there. We see several people we know as we walk up to the door. Some of them are students. Grace sings in the chorus at school, and we see some of the chorus members. I think they might be members of the church's youth choir as well.

As promised, Grace meets us just inside the door and shows us where we should sit. Soon the church pews are packed, and then the lights are lowered in the sanctuary. As it turns out, the choral students we saw outside are not in the program. They have obviously come to hear Grace, who sings a solo. Her voice is impressive. I had no idea she could sing like that. I have heard our high school chorus a few times and knew she was in it, but I did not know she was so talented.

"Did you know she could sing like that?" I ask Todd.

"No! I knew she sang in the chorus but hadn't heard her sing a solo."

Every time I see Grace, I am impressed with her, but also have mixed feelings. Since she and Juan have started spending more time together, he seems to have grown stronger. I don't know if he is actually better, or whether she just gives him the strength to face his challenges. I am glad for that, but it also makes me feel very inadequate. Why can't I be strong and give others strength? Why am I such a wimp?

A little later in the program, Grace sings "O Holy Night," which is my favorite Christmas song. I can't believe I came here not knowing that she is such a great musician.

After Grace's solo, the lady in charge announces a brief "stand up and stretch" break before the next part of the program. I turn to Sophie.

"Did you know Grace can sing like that?"

"Yeah, she's always been good. But she didn't go to our school until senior high. She went to some private Christian school before she came here, I think, but I can't remember where it was."

The last part of the program is beginning, and the choir and the orchestra members are entering the stage again. The whole choir sings several carols, inviting us to sing along with them. I always love that part. They end the program with several songs by a trio in which Grace sings the lead parts. When the program is over, a bunch of us from school hang around so that we can congratulate Grace for her outstanding performance. When Juan comes down the aisle in "Betty," we congratulate him too. Then we all go to Eddie's to get something to eat. Eddie's is a local restaurant that has been around all my life and is a favorite hangout in our town. Juan loves their soft bread pretzels, and Sophie loves their wings.

There is a large crowd when we arrive, so we have to wait a few minutes before a table clears that will seat all 10 or so of us. Finally, a big table opens up. Grace squeezes in beside Juan, and I sit next to Sophie. Most of the talk is about the program, and everyone is telling Grace what a wonderful job she did.

Sophie seems so happy and relaxed that I have almost forgotten about all her troubles at home. When we get up to leave, she hangs back with me as we walk, and I can tell she wants to say something without the others hearing.

"Alice, is it okay if I plan to pick up those things on Friday?" she asks.

"Sure, that's fine. Just call me that morning, so Mom or I will be home. Most any time will be good."

CHAPTER 12

This week is a whirlwind of activity for my family. Every day is filled with shopping; cooking; and talking to my cousins, aunts, and grandparents about Christmas plans. Suddenly it's Friday, and Christmas is two days away. I have not seen or talked to any of my friends since Sunday night, but on Friday morning Sophie calls.

"Can I come by sometime today and pick up those gifts for Joline? Maybe a little before lunch?"

"Sure, I'll be home all day. Just come on over."

When she arrives, I can tell Sophie is a little embarrassed, so I try not to make a big deal of the presents.

"Have you seen any of our gang since last Sunday?" I ask.

"Not really. I saw Grace at the grocery store Monday, but we were both in a hurry."

"Grace was awesome in the program, wasn't she?"

Without answering, Sophie picks up a few of the packages in the corner of the living room. I sense she isn't really thinking about what I said about Grace. I get the rest of the gifts and we head out to the car.

"What are you doing for Christmas?" she asks.

"We usually go to our Christmas Eve service, and then open our gifts when we get home," I answer, trying to judge what my words might sound like to her.

"What do you do on Christmas Day?" she asks.

I get the feeling she may be wanting ideas about what a "normal" family would do.

"My grandmother lives in Nashville, so we usually go visit there on Christmas Day and then stay overnight."

I don't ask Sophie what her family is doing.

Before she leaves, she says, "Say a little prayer for us this weekend. My mom is worried about how things will go with us all together for several days."

"I will," I promise, as I help her place the packages in the car *and* wonder what Grace would say to make Sophie feel better.

"I don't know how to thank you for all you've done to help me lately," she says as she gets in the car.

"We all have our problems, Sophie. I may be calling on you next. I'm glad I have been here for you, and I hope I can always be there when you need me."

As she drives off, I really do pray that things will go well for her this weekend. I'm glad that Mom and I helped her buy presents for little Joline.

On Christmas Eve, Mom, Dad, and I go to our church for a service. Then we go home, eat dinner (usually pizza ordered from Dominos), and open our presents from one another. We don't usually buy expensive things, but give things we need. Tonight, I get a set of luggage that I will probably need for college in the fall. I give Mom a necklace she had shown me at the jewelry store a few weeks ago. I always ask her to point out things when we're shopping that she likes, and I choose from those. Dad is harder to buy for, but Mom helped me, and I ordered him a pair of shoes that she said he wanted but wouldn't spend the money to buy.

On Christmas morning, we leave for Nashville to spend time with relatives. Dad's family is small, and both his parents died when I was too young to remember them, but we always celebrate Christmas with Grandma and Grandpa Morgan, my mother's parents. They live in Nashville, so we always drive over there for the day, and visit with them. Grandma is a retired elementary school teacher, and Grandpa is a doctor. He's retired, too, but he practices part-time at a free clinic for people who can't afford to pay.

My mother has a sister who lives in Bowling Green, Kentucky, and her kids are about my age. She has twin daughters a year younger than I am and a son Ken, who is two years older. They're always there at Christmas, too. I especially enjoy Sherri and Shelli. Aunt Barbara and Mom are very close, so most of the time on Christmas we eat lunch, open presents, and the rest of the time my cousins and I compare our lives while Mom and Aunt Barbara catch up on their own lives.

Today, Ken entertains us with stories of his exploits at Belmont University, where he is a music business major. As soon as we finish opening gifts, he goes to the car and comes back with the new guitar he received for Christmas.

"Wow," says Mom. "That's an impressive guitar."

"It had an impressive price tag, too," says Uncle Mack, laughing.

Physically, Uncle Mack is a stark contrast to his son Ken. He is a short, pudgy little man, with a ring of black hair around an otherwise bald head. Ken, on the other hand, is six-feet tall and lanky, with a head of blond, slightly wavy hair. He did get his dad's love of laughter and easygoing nature, though.

Ken has always enjoyed playing the guitar and singing. He hangs out with a lot of guys who play in bands in Nashville. As we all gather around to admire the guitar, Sherri stands next to her big brother, who towers over her.

"Play that song you were playing last night that was written by John Prine," she says.

"Which one? I played more than one by him."

"I think it was called 'Hello' or something like that."

"'Hello in There'," Ken recalls.

"Yeah, that's it," Shelli chimes in.

Ken starts to play and sing the song, and the twins sing along. I've heard it before, but had never listened to the lyrics much. As he sings, it reminds me a little of Grandma and Grandpa.

When the song is finished, Shelli asks Ken, "Can you take us downtown to one of the places you go all the time?"

"I don't know if they'd be open on Christmas evening," he responds. "Let me check."

He pulls out his cell phone and looks for a few minutes, and then tells us: "One of the restaurants is open, but I don't know if Mom or Aunt Prue would want you 'kids' going there or not." He looks over at Mom and winks.

"Oh, we can go if we're with Ken, can't we Mom?" Sherri stands up and moves toward her mom as if to urge her to agree.

"I guess it's okay. But you girls stay close to Ken, okay?" Mom nods in agreement.

The idea of going to a new place and meeting or seeing lots of new people brings a knot to my stomach. I swallow hard and try not to act like I don't want to go.

"Come on, Alice. Let's go get ready," says Shelli, starting down the hall behind Sherri.

I head down the hallway behind them. They are both dressed in black slacks and silky looking blouses. Sherri's is a beautiful Christmas red, and Shelli's is a Kentucky Wildcats color of blue. Their blouses accentuate their glossy, dark brown hair. The three of us share a room at Grandma's, so it's a little crowded with all of us opening our suitcases and trying to decide whether to change clothes or just freshen our makeup. They had spent Christmas Eve there, so their clothes are already scattered around the room. They decide to wear what they have on, so I do the same.

I'm watching them for cues. I don't wear much makeup or wear fancy clothes, so I say to Sherri as I'm looking down at my gray slacks and black sweater, "I look drab compared to you."

I used to be the one they looked up to, because I was older, but now I feel insecure.

"Oh, you're fine. Wait... let me put just a bit of blush on you to make your cheeks look a little brighter." She grabs a brush and applies the blush, then stands back and admires her handiwork. "Oh yes, that looks great!"

We pile into Ken's blue Honda. Sherri is in the front with Ken, and Shelli and I in the back.

"This is so exciting," says Sherri. "Will any of your friends be there?"

"Probably not, but several of us go there a lot when school is in session. And some of us played there the weekend before Christmas break. Why do you ask? Are you hoping to find a boyfriend? I don't think you should hang out with any of those guys."

"She'd better not be," says Shelli. "Her boyfriend will be furious."

"He's not really my boyfriend," Sherri points out.

"Well, don't tell him that. He's telling all his friends you are," says Shelli.

"Maybe you'd better tell your big brother all about it," says Ken.

"It's just a new boy I've gone to the movies with a few times," says Sherri. "Shelli's the one who really has a boyfriend. They've been dating all year."

I listen as they reveal that Shelli is dating a boy Ken remembers from their school.

It doesn't help me to learn that they are both dating this year. They are juniors. Although I don't really want a boyfriend, it makes me feel like I am behind because my younger cousins have managed to get boyfriends. I can't decide whether to be happy for them, or to feel bad about myself.

"Well, Alice, are you free to look for a boyfriend?" asks Ken. "Looks like my sisters are already committed."

"You said we shouldn't hang out with any of your friends," Shelli reminds him.

"I didn't say Alice shouldn't. I just said you shouldn't. Alice is a senior this year, so she's at a different stage in life."

We all laugh, and I'm glad he remembers that I'm the older one of the cousins. It makes me feel better.

When we get to the restaurant, we have a tough time finding a parking space, which is surprising on Christmas evening, but it's full of young, college-age people. Ken doesn't seem to recognize anyone.

The menu contains mostly burgers of all kinds, with a few other sandwiches thrown in. It is a welcome relief from all the turkey and dressing and other typical Christmas dishes we've been having the last few weeks.

I notice they are setting up for live music, so I ask Ken, "Who are the musicians tonight?"

"I have no idea," he answers, just as a young man comes up from behind him and stops at our table.

"Hey man, what are you doing here?" the guy says.

"My grandparents live here," Ken says. "These are my twin sisters, Sherri and Shelli. And this is my cousin Alice."

"Didn't know you had all these beautiful relatives, or I would have treated you better," the guy says, laughing. "Girls, my name is Leonardo. I'm Ken's really good friend. I'm also in some classes with him at Belmont and have played in a band with him on some occasions."

It's obvious we are all impressed with Leonardo. No one says anything for a moment, and then Shelli recovers and asks, "What do you play?"

"I play the mandolin."

What do you say to a mandolin player?

"Wow. That's interesting. Are you playing tonight?" Sherri asks.

"As a matter of fact, I am. We're getting started in just a few minutes. I hope you will stay."

"Who are you playing with tonight?" asks Ken.

"It's a new group, made up of pieces of two separate groups."

Ken and his friend talk about one of the bands for a few minutes before Leonardo has to go on over to where they will be playing. Before he leaves, he says, "By the way, I'll be needing one of your beautiful ladies to come onto the stage with me for one of the songs. I think it's the third or fourth one. You all decide which one wants to do it."

As Leonardo walks away, the three of us look at one another. I can tell both Sherri and Shelli want to be the chosen one, but I am petrified at the thought. Then Ken says, "I nominate Alice."

"No, no. It's okay. Sherri, you do it."

We go back and forth a bit, and by the time the band starts, we have not made a definite decision. My stomach is churning.

During the second song, I think I'm going to be sick. I announce to my cousins, "I'm going to the restroom. If I'm not back, one of you just go on up there when he asks for someone."

I stay in the restroom through the song, and listen to see if Leonardo calls for someone to come up for the third song. He doesn't, so I stay through it too. I wait until they start the fourth song to leave the restroom. Then, I just stand outside the door until I'm sure Sherri or Shelli has gone up on the stage, but I can't see the stage clearly.

I walk over to where I can see our table, and I see that Shelli is still there. She sees me and motions for me to come over and sit down, and we listen to the rest of the song. It includes a short dialogue with Sherri where Leonardo pretends to ask her for a date, and she accepts. It's all fun, and she enjoys it. I'm glad she does. To me, it's just a good show and I like listening to the band.

When we get back in the car, Shelli asks, "Alice, did you not want to go up on the stage at all?"

"No, I didn't. I would have been scared to death."

"I didn't realize you were so shy. It was fun. I loved it!" Sherri says.

"If I'd known you didn't want to do it, I wouldn't have 'nominated' you," Ken said. "I knew Sherri and Shelli would both want to do it, so I just wanted to give you a chance."

I didn't want him to think I didn't appreciate what he'd said. "I know, and I do appreciate it. I'm just too shy. I've been trying to improve, but I would have been terrified to go up on that stage."

The experience made me realize that, although I've made some progress in overcoming my shyness, I still have a long way to go.

"Is Leonardo in the music business program too?" Sherri asks.

"No, I think he's a science major. He just likes music, so he hangs around with us a lot. He's a nice guy, not like some of the others."

"What does that mean?" asks Shelli.

"Well, he just seems a little more grounded. He lives here in Nashville, and his parents teach religion and philosophy at Belmont."

After we get back to Grandma's and report about our night out, the girls and I go into our room and talk for an hour or so, while the adults clean up the kitchen from their dinner and continue to visit.

Finally, it's time for bed, but we keep talking until midnight. I'm glad we've had this time together. When the lights are out, I lie awake a while and think back over the day. Before I go to sleep, I wonder what Christmas has been like for Sophie and Juan.

I picture Sophie trying to protect Joline from the arguing going on between their parents. Then I try to picture some form of reconciliation between her parents. Maybe her dad agrees to go into rehab for his alcoholism. I'm not real optimistic that anything like that will happen, based on what Sophie has told me.

Then I think about Juan. I wonder if he has spent the day with his godparents or with his mother and brothers. He didn't say anything about what he planned to do. I think his godparents' home would be more pleasant for him, but I think he probably would want to be with his brothers. He says very little about his family. I've heard others say negative things about his mother, but he usually takes up for her. He is always concerned about his brothers. I try to imagine what it would be like for him, spending the day with his brothers. I can see him rough-housing with the little ones and laughing with them. I wonder if they received presents. I wonder what they had for Christmas dinner. Juan's world is so different from mine that I can't really picture what they might do on Christmas Day.

Soon I fall into a deep sleep and awake to the whispering of Sherri and Shelli trying to gather their belongings and get on the road. I lift my head sleepily and say, "Good morning, girls."

"We were trying not to wake you," says Sherri.

"And not say goodbye?" I ask, sitting up and pulling my covers up around me.

"We've really enjoyed visiting with you," Shelli adds. "We need to get together more."

I agree, but it may be even more difficult once I'm in college. I grab my robe and follow them into the kitchen, where Mom and Aunt Barbara are having a cup of coffee with Grandma, and Dad and Uncle Mack are coming in from taking a load of luggage to the car.

"Where is Ken?" I ask.

"He's still asleep. He's not going back with us. He's staying in Nashville. He has an apartment over near Belmont," says Aunt Barbara. "He'll probably be eating over here with you a lot, Mom." They both laugh.

Soon the twins and their parents get everything together and head back to Bowling Green, and we close the living room door and go back toward the kitchen.

"Now, maybe I'll get some of your attention," says Grandma, patting me on the shoulder as she follows me. I turn and give her a hug. I realize I have barely talked to my grandparents since arriving here.

"I'm sorry, Grandma. I didn't mean to ignore you."

"I know, honey. You girls all like to talk to each other. I'm glad you enjoy being together. I do want to hear everything about you, though. How's your school year going?"

"It's fine."

"Are you still debating this year?"

I nod, and then Grandma looks at Mom and asks with a smile on her face, "Is she always this talkative?"

"Pretty much. She's working on it, though. She's got to get ready for college, you know. She's making progress. Aren't you, Alice?"

"I hope so."

"Mom, Alice is a leader in many ways, even though she doesn't talk much. She has friends who rely on her to help them. I'm so proud of all she does to support the friends who need her. Did we tell you that one of her best friends is a young man who has lost both a leg and an arm because of cancer?"

"No! That's so sad, Alice. I know he appreciates your friendship."

"It's not really like that, Grandma. He has more friends than I do. And he helps me a lot more than I help him."

"Maybe you're like me. I was kind of shy, but I had friends," Grandma says knowingly.

I always like being at Grandma's house. I feel loved and accepted. I am reluctant to leave the safety and comfort of her love. All too soon it's noon and we are making turkey and ham sandwiches, and dragging out the potato salad and sweet tea. Ken has finally awakened and come down for a late breakfast.

"I've got to go now, Grandma. I'll try to come back in a few days, maybe this weekend."

"Aw, Ken, why don't you just stay here until school starts back?" urges Grandpa.

"I've got to get back to the apartment. My roommate is coming back this evening, too, and we may book a gig or two to make a little spending money this week."

"Okay, come on back any time. You know you're always welcome," says Grandpa, as Ken carries his bag out the door.

When we finish lunch, Mom and Grandma start to put up the leftovers while Dad begins packing the car.

"Alice, get your stuff together and I'll start putting things in the car. We need to head back to Closeville soon," says Dad.

As I pack my suitcase, I notice something shiny on the bed and realize Sherri has left a pair of earrings lying there. It was still a little dark in the room when they left, but now with the overhead light on, the earrings are easy to see. I remember seeing them sparkling on stage last night. It reminds me of how confident she seemed. That's my goal: to do something like that and not be afraid. I start to place the earrings on the dresser up close to the mirror, but then I decide to put them on. In seconds I feel different, more confident. I tilt my head a bit so they jiggle and sparkle, just as they did on Sherri last night. I know I wouldn't have felt that way last night, but now they are like magic.

Meanwhile, Mom enters the doorway. "Are you ready? What are you doing?"

I am startled. "I found Sherri's earrings on the bed and decided to try them on. What do you think? Do they look good on me?"

"Of course. They're beautiful. Are you taking them with you?"

"No. She might be back before we are. Or she might even ask Grandma to mail them to her."

"Okay. Come on then. We're ready to go."

As Mom turns to leave the room, I take off the earrings, silently bidding them goodbye and thanking them for giving my confidence a boost.

By the time we arrive back in Closeville, it is almost dinnertime, so we drive through Wendy's and pick up burgers on the way into town. Although I am anxious to learn how Sophie and Juan spent Christmas, I am tired and decide I'll wait until tomorrow to call them.

CHAPTER 13

After spending the night away from home, I am always glad to be back in my own bed. I crack open one of the books I received for Christmas, but soon my eyes get heavy, so I turn off my light.

Suddenly, I hear my phone ringing and realize that I have been asleep, and it is daylight outside. I can't remember where my phone is for a moment. It seems to be on my bed somewhere. I remember texting Sherri when we got home. By the time I pick the phone up, it has rung three or four times. I look at it and see that it is Juan. That's really unusual. He usually just texts me.

"Hello." My voice is just a mumble, not ready to get up yet.

"Alice?" Juan sounds wide awake, but troubled.

"Yes," more awake now. "Are you okay?"

"Well, no. I mean, I am but…" He stops, and for a moment I think he will cry. "Carlos tried to kill himself." Carlos is 16.

I am fully awake now and inquire, "Where are you?"

"I'm at home, at my godmother's. But she had to go to work this morning."

"I'll be right over," I assure him.

I put my clothes on quickly and run downstairs, where Mom and Dad are finishing breakfast. I tell them what Juan said. "I'm going over to his house. I think Juan needs a friend with him."

"Is there anything we can do?" asks Mom.

"I doubt it, but I'll call you when I learn more details."

As I drive to Juan's house, I think how honored I feel that he called me. I think of all the people he has encouraged and helped, and of all those who have helped him. Juan has lots of friends, both his age and adults who would come to his aid if he had asked. Why did he choose to call me?

When I arrive at Juan's house, the front door is cracked a little. I push it open. "Juan?"

"Over here," he says.

I look toward the corner of the large room and see him sitting in his wheelchair. I have never seen him so down. I have the urge to give him a hug, so I put my arm around his shoulders for a moment, then sit down on the couch near his chair and wait. He doesn't say anything for maybe a whole minute.

"I have been fighting for my life for five years," he says. "Why does my brother, who is healthy and well, want to end his? It just doesn't make sense."

"You're right. It doesn't."

We sit in silence for a few minutes, and then I ask, "Would it help if I called Brother Adams?" Adams is the pastor of Grace's church. "Would you like to talk to him?"

"Yes, I would. He might help me sort it out."

While we wait for Brother Adams, we say very little. I wish I knew something wise to say, but about all I can do is get a Coke for Juan and ask him if he's eaten anything. He says he hasn't, so I bring him a Pop Tart I found in the kitchen cabinet.

Within an hour after I call Brother Adams, he is at Juan's door. The presence of this tall, heavy-set, kind man fills the room both physically and emotionally as soon as he enters.

"Thank you for coming," Juan says to the pastor.

I tell Juan that I'll let them talk, and if he needs me to call, and I head back home.

When I get home, Mom asks, "How is Juan?"

"I've never seen him so upset. He seems to be particularly upset because he has fought so hard to live, and his brother doesn't want to live. I had no idea what to say to him. I called Brother Adams for him, and he came over. I hope he will know how to talk to Juan about it."

"You did the right thing," Mom assures me. "Brother Adams may think a little differently about suicide than the Catholic priest would, too. He might be able to comfort Juan more than the priest would."

In the following days, I talk a little with Juan, and he says that Brother Adams is helping him work through the trauma of his brother's actions. He doesn't tell me much, but he says that the pastor focuses on the forgiving nature of God. By the end of our Christmas break, Juan seems a little better.

CHAPTER 14

As soon as Christmas break is over, I begin to panic about college. I didn't apply for early admission because I don't know what I want to do or what my major will be. I visited several colleges last summer. I have thought about staying close to home and attending Kennesaw State University or Georgia Highlands College until I choose a major. I think I'd like to do something in communications, but I'm afraid I can't do well since I am so shy. I love to write, and I think I will do well with an application essay, but they may want me to come for an interview and I'm not sure about that. I am beginning to be a little more at ease though, so maybe if I can find a part of the communications program that focuses more on writing I could do it. Regular admission deadlines are coming up next month, so I've got to get busy. Mom said she'd help me tonight after dinner.

"Okay, do you still want to talk about college tonight?" she says, as we finish eating.

"I guess so." I sigh. "I don't know what to do or where to start."

"Well, it's your decision, but maybe we can talk a little about the options. I know you aren't sure about a major, but since you like writing, let's start with that. Also, think about the colleges you've visited and which ones you liked best. Maybe you can pick two or three to apply to in the next few weeks."

We review the materials I have, and I decide to apply to Kennesaw and West Georgia, which are close by, and to Auburn University in Alabama. I feel better after making a plan for the applications.

The next day I decide to talk to the school counselor, Ms. Willoughby. She is easy to talk to and always immensely helpful, no matter what the problem is. She knows everything about Closeville High School. She has been working there ever since I was a little girl. I would go to school with Mom during teacher work days when I was in 1st grade, and Ms. Willoughby would give me candy or gum and make me feel special. Over the years I've been in her office many times, even before I started high school. In the last two years she has often helped Juan by taking him to his cancer treatments and visiting him in the hospital. Juan depends on her a lot to make arrangements for his appointments when his godmother has to work or do something else and can't go with him.

When I enter her office, Ms. Willoughby comes out from behind her desk and gives me a hug. "To what do I owe the honor of a visit from you today?" she asks.

That's a typical greeting from Ms. Willoughby. I always feel special when I'm with her, but I think she makes the other students feel the same way.

"I need to get my college applications in, and I thought you could help me."

"I sure can. Have you decided on where you want to go?"

"Not really, but I've decided to apply to Kennesaw and West Georgia, which are close by, and to Auburn in Alabama. Do you think that sounds okay?"

"Of course. Whatever you decide is fine. Why Auburn?"

"I read where they have an exploratory program where you don't have to declare a major the first year, and your advisors help you investigate different possibilities."

"I guess that means you don't have a clue what your major will be." Ms. Willoughby laughs. "You'd be surprised how many other students have the same problem, especially the really smart ones like yourself. They make good grades in everything and love learning, so they like to study a lot of different things."

"Oh, I never thought of it like that," I admit. "I just thought I was dumb because so many others know what they want to major in before they go to college."

"Some people just love one thing, such as math or science, and that's okay. But many students are like you. I want you to understand that the world is wide open, and you have many choices."

Ms. Willoughby and I look at each college's requirements for application, and she prints them out for me. She suggests that I go through all of them with Mom and then come back with any questions I have. Of course, I looked at some of the stuff last summer, but I hadn't paid close attention to any of it. Now I realize how much work I have to do before actually submitting the three applications. I know that I'll have to write an essay for Auburn's application. I also want to apply for scholarships if they are available, especially at Auburn, since out-of-state tuition always costs more.

The next few days I spend every spare moment on the applications. They keep me busy and a little less panicky since I'm making progress. The more I learn about Auburn, the more I hope I get accepted there. At the same time, I'm a little scared about the whole idea of going away to college.

As I look through the materials I have found about the different colleges, I find a very rough version of an application essay I started last fall. In it I had focused on experiences I thought were unique. From what we can tell at this point, Auburn is the only one of the three colleges where I've applied that requires a supplemental essay, and none of them require the SAT with the essay. I'll get more details as I go along. I need to talk to Ms. Willoughby about the exact requirements for the supplemental essay.

CHAPTER 15

Now that we are all filling out college applications and applying for scholarships, the days and weeks are so full that I am stressed out all the time. I realize that I am neglecting Juan, and I know that he is still feeling a little down because of what happened with his brother during Christmas break.

"How is Carlos?" I ask one afternoon when we are talking on the phone.

"He seems much better. Did I tell you that I got him to go talk to Brother Adams with me last week?"

"No, I didn't know about that."

"It was Grace who suggested it. I was afraid that Carlos wouldn't go with me, but he did. Anyway, it went really well, and Carlos went back by himself the next day. I think that was part of his problem. He had no adults to talk to about his feelings."

Although, Juan never reveals the nature of Carlos' problems, I think he feels good about his progress at this point.

Juan has reminded me that the state playoffs for the girls' basketball team start this weekend. Last year when the girls won region, that was all they talked about. I just know Sophie is excited.

Later in the day when I see her, I congratulate her on her team's win.

"Yeah, we won. We always win. The playoffs start in two weeks."

"Last year you said it had been 20 years since the girls' team had won region," I remind her.

"Well, yeah, but I mean our team—we always win."

"Okay. Anyway, I'm happy for you."

Why is it that things become commonplace so quickly?

"Are you coming to the playoffs this weekend?" Sophie asks me this evening as we prepare for our next debate tournament.

"I think so. Mom said we'd go, at least on the first night. Juan and Todd may ride with us, and I think Isabella and Ms. Lucas are coming too."

"That's great. You all are kind of like family to me."

"We've all got to stick together." I don't know what else to say to her because I know she wishes her own family would support her more.

The thing is, all of us need each other in some way. We have our difficulties, but in the end, we care enough to support one another. Even though all of us help

Juan a lot, he helps us as much or more. If any of us need a boost, he's always there to cheer us up. That's what makes me worry about him when he's down, like he was right after Christmas. I am so thankful for Brother Adams because I had no clue how to encourage Juan that day, but Brother Adams did.

On Friday, our team plays at 7:00 p.m. at Parkview High School. We are leaving early enough to stop in Kennesaw and eat something. Ms. Lucas and Isabella will join us.

At Chick-fil-A, Isabella and I order sandwiches, Mom and Ms. Lucas order salads, and Juan and Todd both get a large order of chicken strips and fries.

"I'm starved," says Todd. "It's been a long time since lunch."

"You're always hungry," says Juan. "Remember that time you ate three hot dogs, one right after another, and then got sick?" They both laugh at the memory. "I will never forget that. It was right before your first basketball game of the season when we were freshmen. I laughed until I cried."

"I know. I learned my lesson though—never did that again!"

When we pull into the parking lot at the school, Mom tries to find a place close to the gym to make it easier for Juan—although he wouldn't want that, as he doesn't want to be treated as an invalid. We end up having to park a long way from the entrance, so Todd pushes Juan's wheelchair and we all go in together.

When we go to her games, we usually try to sit where she can see us when her team comes out to warm up. Tonight, though, it will be difficult because there is a large crowd in the gym. I finally see some spaces really close where Juan can sit beside us in his wheelchair. The team is coming on the floor now, and I see Sophie looking around a little, but I can't tell whether she sees us or not. Maybe she does. I hope so.

I think the teams are well matched, but I don't know if that's good or not. I ask Todd what he thinks about our chances, and he just shrugs. Coach Callahan is talking to the girls and getting them ready for the game. I go to a lot of the games, but I still have trouble understanding some of the rules, so I have to rely on Todd sometimes to understand why a player is fouled or some other call is made.

During the first quarter our team looks good, keeping ahead most of the time. At half-time the score is tied, so we're optimistic. But soon after the second half starts, we lag behind. And at the end we lose by 15 points.

On the way home from the game, Juan asks, "Are either of you going on a senior trip after graduation?"

"Not me," answers Todd. "I'll have to work all summer and save money for college."

"I don't know." I remember that Juan's GoFund Me account was set up to help him do some fun things. Ms. Lucas had said that one thing on his list was to go to Mexico. I can't remember if he has ever been, since his mother is from there, or if perhaps he went there when he was really young. Anyway, I thought that Isabella had said something while on our trip to California about us all going to Cancun after graduation. But I'm afraid to mention it in case we can't do it now. I'll ask Mom if she knows of any plans being made for such a trip.

When I ask her, Mom says she isn't aware of a trip to Cancun. "Martha Lucas is the one you need to ask. I guess if any of you are going, though, we need to make plans."

When I see Isabella the next week, she says that her mother had mentioned it the day before. "Will you go with us?" she asks. "I was thinking that Mom and Ms. Willoughby might let Grace, you, and me go with Juan. I don't know if anyone else would want to go with us. What about Sophie? Would she want to go?"

"Maybe. Should I ask her?"

"Sure. Why not?"

"I'll talk to her the next time I see her," I tell Isabella.

Chapter 16

This weekend will be our last debate tournament, and I am not looking forward to it. The debate team has been my whole life for the last four years, and I'm sad that it's coming to an end. All three of our teams are going and I'm glad. I don't want Mom to notice that I'm upset. I doubt that the others feel this way. The tournament will be at Grovetown High School, and since it is both Friday and Saturday, we will stay overnight at a hotel.

"It's a good thing we're spending the night," says Todd. "I hear it's going to be stormy this evening."

"Really?" Sophie asks. "I hope we don't have a tornado."

"It may not even rain," says Bert. "We used to have a lot of tornadoes when we lived in Arkansas. We got used to it, though. We never had any damage, but our neighbors lost everything one time when a tornado came through our community."

When we get to the tournament and I talk to a few other students, I realize that the resolution for this month is more controversial than I had realized. Most people probably think that all topics are controversial, and they are in a way, but this one is different. The resolution states, "Resolved: the U.S. should no longer pressure Israel to work toward a two-state solution."

I didn't know that some students are so emotional about this topic until we got here. No one on our team reacted to it any differently than any of the other topics. It is very personal with some of the kids here. Many of them seem to be frustrated that we are even debating the issue. They say that their parents believe we should always support Israel. But some politicians have not pressured Israel to work toward a two-state solution anyway. The tension about the resolution makes me a little nervous. Usually, Sophie and I spend time together before pairings come out and also sit together in the van, but not this time. She's talking to Jason as if their lives depend on winning strategies in this debate. I guess they're just all glad that this is our last tournament.

In debate we usually laugh about the two different sides of our topic and don't have much personal involvement, but this time it's different. Todd and I present our Con position brief first, and I can tell that our opponents have strong feelings about the topic. It isn't our average debate for sure. Tempers flare and I can tell that our opponents aren't merely reading a brief. They are serious. I also notice a political divide at this tournament.

I cite evidence that any U.S. pressure on Israel at this time is minimal at best, and it is not enough to damage relations. I argue that in the status quo, the U.S. is merely keeping the two-state option open and might encourage Israel to keep an open mind to it. I also argue that completely abandoning any hope for this solution would disrupt the ongoing peace process, which has prevented open conflict in the area, even if it does not result in the formation of two states.

The first Pro speaker begins by saying that any pressure on Israel for a two-state solution is bad for U.S./Israel relations. He continues by making the general argument that we should just abandon this idea because it will inevitably fail and is creating a mental block to possible practical alternatives. As we expected, he also mentions that a two-state solution would be bad for security.

When it is Todd's turn to speak, he begins by refuting the Pro position that a two-state solution would be bad for security by pointing out that the argument is only relevant if this solution materializes. The Pro speaker had argued that they did not believe this could ever materialize. Todd continues by saying that keeping the idea on the table will prevent a breakdown in peace talks even if it does not lead to a two-state solution. He says that rather than creating a mental block to other alternatives, it may keep the door open for thinking of practical alternatives.

We struggle through the rebuttals and the crossfire questions, but Todd and I are fortunate this time to have been able to present a strong Con position. From all the evidence we read, the fact that there is little, if any, pressure being put on Israel now makes the Pro position more difficult to argue. We did find some support, but it is difficult to construct arguments to support a resolution recommending the end of something that seems to have already been stopped!

When the round is over, Todd and the rest of our team head out to get a snack. I look for Sophie, but she is nowhere to be found. She seems to be avoiding me today. I don't know what's wrong with her. I talk to a girl I met from Grovetown High School for a few minutes and then go back to where the boys are. Juan and Bert tell me about their last round.

"I'm pretty sure we won," says Bert. "I'm glad we did not have to argue the Pro position."

"I think we could have won, anyway," says Juan. "We're just better than they are, Bert."

"Maybe… But our Pro position is not as strong as our Con. There's just not that many arguments to make for the resolution. Besides, why are we even debating this anyway? The United States is not even pressuring Israel toward a two-state resolution."

"Do you get the idea that there's a lot of tension about this topic—more than usual?" I ask. "It's like we're arguing, not debating."

"Yes! I heard this girl say that her mother told her not to argue against supporting Israel," says Juan. "I don't know how you'd promise something like that."

"Yeah," agrees Bert. "You might have to drop out of debate if you couldn't argue both sides of something. Of course, this topic is not really for or against Israel. It's just talking about U.S. policy."

Bert's family is Jewish, and they have been to Israel several times. His dad does not agree with some of Israel's policies, but some members of his congregation always criticize him when he expresses it. Bert is really smart. He and Jason are a lot alike in many ways. I don't think Bert is quite as competitive as Jason, though. And unlike Jason, Bert hardly ever says anything to offend others. He knows how to relate to people.

I remember a conversation my parents had the other day. "Mom says that most people don't understand how complicated Middle-Eastern problems are. From what little I've read, I think she's right."

"What did you read?" Bert asks.

"I read this book called *The Lemon Tree* by Sandy Tolan. It's about an Arab guy and a Jewish woman who had lived in the same house at different times when they were children. They meet and learn about their past. When I finished the book, I kept wondering if there is any way these people can ever learn to live together in peace. I decided that the only way they could is if one side decides to give up something. But that doesn't seem likely, does it?"

"Who do you think is right?" asks Jason. "The Arabs or the Jews?"

I hesitate a moment. "I honestly don't know. In some ways they're both right, and in some ways they're both wrong. That's why the only way to peace is for someone to give up something."

"Don't you think that's the way it is with all of us?" observes Juan. "We just have to be responsible for the way we treat others. We're all good in some ways and bad in others. Lots of people around here don't like me because I'm Mexican, but I can't help where my mother was born. All I can control is what I do and how I treat other people."

"You are so right, man," says Bert, looking at Juan. "Look at you. You've got all kinds of reasons to be grumpy, but you aren't—at least most of the time." He laughs.

Finally, it is the last round of the day, and Todd and I have been lucky so far. We have debated Con in all the rounds, and we've got our case down well. But this time we must debate Pro. Since we haven't had to debate that position, we haven't improved what we started out with. We have, of course, seen our opponents struggle with it, so we've learned a few things. In the short prep time before we begin, we make several changes that might help, and we go into the round confident.

In debate it's important to sound like you know what you're talking about— whether you do or not. I'm listening to Todd, and I begin to think we're doing okay. But when our opponent's second speaker gets up to speak, I'm not so sure. The round goes quickly, and when it's over, Todd and I agree that it's a toss-up. We did better than we might have with a stronger team, but they made some compelling arguments too.

As soon as the last round is over, we load into the van and start looking for somewhere to eat. We agree to stop at Wendy's. Mom reminds us that we have to be on the debate floor by 8 a.m., so we get our food quickly and then head to the hotel after 10 o'clock.

Meanwhile, Todd is checking the weather app on his phone. "They're talk-ing about stormy weather and possible tornadoes on my weather app, but I don't know if it's near here."

We are almost at our hotel, so none of the rest of us have time to check any-thing. As soon as Mom gets us checked in and gives us our keys, we head to our rooms. We are on the second floor and have three adjoining rooms, with Sophie and me on one side of Mom, and the guys on the other.

After we get settled in and I am about to put on my pajamas, we hear a knock. When we open the door, it's a staff member telling us a tornado has been spotted about an hour from us and we should go to the first floor. Before we get out the door, all the lights go off—pitch-black dark!

"Does anyone have a flashlight?" The answer is no. Sophie says she has one on her phone, but she left it in the room where she had placed it on the charger, and the same is true of two or three others. After a quick "survey," we find that none of the rest of us have anything to provide light either. After our day at the tournament, most of our phone batteries are down or the phones are still in our rooms. Mom's phone light helps a little. We all huddle together and shuffle down the stairs, trying not to fall. Todd folds Juan's wheelchair and maneuvers it down the steps. Bert is in front of Juan and Jason is behind him as he hops along, hold-ing to the rail.

We finally get to the bottom of the stairs and try to decide which way to go. Juan gets back in his wheelchair, and Bert is pushing him. We're walking along an outside sidewalk beside the hotel and then in a kind of courtyard. In the dimness, I can see some other guests walking ahead of us and some coming toward us. A few of the guests say they are going to one of the downstairs rooms where they know other guests.

Jason is trying to give us a lecture about the different types of tornadoes, and I am a little afraid now because the wind is blowing more fiercely than before. By accident, I guess, we see a faint glint of light and stumble into the lobby of the hotel, which is filled with other guests sitting on the floor. I believe some of them are students from the debate tournament, but it's hard to tell.

A tall man, a hotel staff person I assume, is standing at the desk checking his phone constantly. I hear someone say we are "in its path." I assume they mean the tornado. Tired voices ask questions of the tall man periodically, and he tries to answer. We sit there for what seems like at least 30 minutes, and then his phone rings and a decided hush falls over the crowd as he answers.

"I understand," he says after a few seconds. "Yes, the board room is best I think." I begin to hear what seems to be a roar, and then remember reading about the sound a tornado makes.

He punches the off button on the phone and then urges, "I think it best if we relocate down the hall in our board room. There are a lot of windows and glass doors in here."

As we begin to stand, a lady gathers her two small children and moves down the hall, I hear one of the children start to cry, and the other one asks, "Will we be blown away, Mommy?"

"No, dear. We're going to a safer room," she answers.

When we get to the board room, it seems more crowded than the lobby, but there are only a few windows, and just the one door, which the tall man closes. We get settled on the floor as close to Juan's wheelchair as we can, and I notice that Mom has made sure we are all in a huddle. She looks a little worried.

Sophie gets as close to Mom as she can, and for a moment I think she might cry. Then she looks at me and seems to purposely straighten her back and smile. "We'll have an adventure to tell tomorrow."

"Yeah, if we live to tell it…," adds Jason.

"Don't say that," says Juan. "We'll be fine. I just said my prayers. The Bible says the prayers of a righteous man…"

"And what does that have to do with you, man?" inquires Todd.

The exchange breaks the tension, and they both laugh softly. But you can tell we are all a little rattled by the seriousness of the moment. The roaring continues, and I feel as if we are all holding our collective breaths for several minutes. I don't know exactly how long this goes on, but it seems like forever. Finally, silence falls over the room and the tall man tells us to stay put for a few minutes while he checks the premises.

He isn't gone too long, and we are a little more relaxed when he returns. After talking to those inside and outside the hotel and in the surrounding area, he learns that except for a small area at the far side of the hotel, it has suffered no damage. The hotel staff will relocate people who are staying in four rooms on the second and third floors on that side, but otherwise no damage has been done.

The electricity comes back on at about 1 a.m. We all start texting our families. Apparently, Dad is sitting by his phone waiting for word when Mom calls. He has read that the National Weather Service reported damage in Grovetown. Several frame homes, mobile homes, and businesses were damaged.

By 2 o'clock, Sophie and I are in our beds. In what seems like a few minutes, my alarm goes off and it's time to wake up. I can't even remember what we're supposed to debate today, but I muddle through breakfast. After drinking a Diet Coke and eating an egg biscuit, I begin to feel awake.

The 15-minute drive to the school helps me to get back in sync with what I'm supposed to be doing.

"Oh, yes, I remember now. Our debate is about Israel and a two-state solution," I say to Sophie. "Which side are you on?"

"I don't know," she answers. "No one has flipped the coin."

We laugh as we enter the cafeteria to get our pairings.

Today will be okay. I'm not going to worry about winning and losing after surviving last night's storm. I'm just going to do the best I can. I'm not as nervous as I usually am. I may even enjoy the crossfire today. Todd even notices that I don't seem to be uptight in the rounds today.

"Congratulations, Alice," he says. "I think you're winning the battle. You seem almost relaxed today."

"Thank you. Last night I realized there are things more important than what someone thinks of how you answer a crossfire question."

"That was pretty scary, wasn't it?" he says.

"Yeah, I just tried not to think about it, but it was scary, that's for sure."

When we gather back in the school auditorium for the awards, we are a little late getting in there and most of the seats are taken. Mom is standing at the entrance trying to help us find a seat, but we just can't all sit together, so Todd and I end up sitting across the room from the rest of our group.

I always dread this part of debate tournaments because most of the time none of us win awards—well, Jason and Sophie do sometimes, but Todd and I seldom do, and Juan and Bert have had to miss several tournaments.

When the tournament directors start giving out awards, the first names called are Jason and Sophie. A lot of other awards are also given, so Todd and I are just waiting for it to be over. But then we hear the names of Bert and Juan. Next, they call "Alice Jarvis and Todd Hurley." Todd and I stare at each other a moment until we realize the directors are calling our names. When we join the others of our group, Todd says, "Well, that's a first!" "And last!" we all say at the same time. I think that's when it really hits everyone that it's our last debate. It's especially hard because of Juan, but he's in good spirits.

On the way home Mom says, "This is the first time I've had all seniors on the team in a long time. Do you want to have some sort of year-end celebration? If so, what do you want to do? We can have something at my house, or go out to eat together, or do something else if you have an idea."

"We could go out to eat and then go somewhere and watch a movie or something," says Todd.

"Maybe we could go eat at Eddie's and then go over to your house, Mrs. Jarvis, and watch something—and maybe have dessert," suggests Juan.

"Why don't we watch the movie, *The Great Debaters*," says Bert. "Have any of you seen that? It's an old movie, but very good."

"I've heard about it, but not seen it," says Jason.

"Okay, I'll be glad for you to come to our house and watch the movie and eat dessert," says Mom.

I'm looking at my calendar. "Can we do it next weekend—maybe Saturday night?" I ask. "I'll make something for dessert."

"I'm sure my mom would be glad to make a dessert, too," adds Bert.

"I can bring chips," offers Todd.

"I will bring something, but I'm not sure what it will be," says Sophie.

"Same here," agrees Jason.

"I think I can bring something too," Juan chimes in.

Mom looks around. "Looks like we have a plan then. Alice and I will meet you at Eddie's on Saturday night. If any of you need a ride, just let us know."

CHAPTER 17

These days everybody is talking about prom. Sophie and I are sitting on my bed talking about who's going with whom. I'm not sure if I even want to go, but of course Sophie says she wants to go. I can't think of anyone who would ask me. I assume Juan and Grace will go together, and I suspect Jason will ask Sophie.

But Sophie laughs and says, "No, he won't."

"I think he likes you. Besides, no one else would probably go with him. You understand him a little, and appreciate how smart he is."

"You know who he reminds me of a little?" she asks. I shake my head "no."

"Sheldon, on *Big Bang Theory*. Jason is a lot like that. He says the weirdest things. He is very smart in some ways, but he's very stupid too."

"Anyway, if he asks, would you go with him?"

"Yeah, I guess. I don't want to have a boyfriend really. I don't have time for one. I just want to go to the senior prom."

Jason wants to be a professor like his dad, except he wants to teach chemistry. He often gives us "mini lectures" on some aspect of chemistry while we're traveling to and from debate tournaments. Once we were debating something that had to do with the environment, and he got in an argument with one of the judges over some particular fact that she challenged. It got out of hand, and Mom had to intervene. I think he had to sit out for the rest of the tournament. He didn't argue with Mom, though. He just kept quiet and took his punishment.

"Oh, by the way," I say to Sophie when she starts to leave that night, "I think some of us are going to Cancun for our senior trip. Ms. Lucas and Ms. Willoughby will be going with us. Would you want to go?"

"Who all is going?"

"Grace, Juan, Isabella, and I. It's one of the things on Juan's wish list when they started the GoFundMe account. His mother is from Mexico, you know."

Sophie is hesitant. "I'm not sure my mom will let me, but I'll ask her." I get the feeling there might be more to her hesitancy than getting her mom's permission.

"Okay, just let me know. I'll tell you when Ms. Lucas and Ms. Willoughby need to have a commitment from us," I say as Sophie goes out the door.

After a bunch of us have been out to eat one evening, Jason hangs back when we start to leave and asks Sophie, "Could I speak to you a moment?" She stays back to talk to him and later tells me he asked her to the prom. She says he must have rehearsed his "proposal," because he worded it in a very formal way.

"Did you agree to go?" I ask.

"Of course. I told you I wanted to go to the prom." I think he may be more interested in a relationship with Sophie than she realizes, though.

"Are you sure you don't want to go to the prom?" she asks. "If you'd go, maybe the two of us and our dates could do something special such as eat at a nice restaurant or go to an after-prom party."

"No one has asked me," I respond, "and I doubt they will. Who would ask me?"

"I think you're better liked by everyone than you think," Sophie assures me. "Hey, maybe Todd will ask you. That'd be perfect, because he's used to Jason."

"I don't know. I've never thought about going. I doubt Todd will ask me, though. He'll probably ask one of the girls on your basketball team."

After our talk, I start thinking that maybe I should consider going just in case someone asks me.

When I get home, Mom is grading papers in the living room. She looks up when I come in. "Are you going to the prom?" she asks.

"No," and walk on through the room hurriedly so she can't say any more.

It annoys me that Mom asked about the prom, but I'm not sure why. It's a reasonable question. Although she should know that no one has asked me, it is a common thing for students to go without dates. There are plenty of friend groups going to prom without committing to dates. They are simply having fun without that added pressure. I realize after talking to Sophie that I am beginning to wish someone would ask me to the prom. I might enjoy going with Todd because he is probably the only boy besides Juan that I can talk to without getting anxious.

I go upstairs and dig through my backpack for my homework. As I begin my work, my mind goes back to prom. I think about Todd and wonder if he would think about asking me to go with him. Although I don't think he will, I've decided that if he does, I'll say yes.

Suddenly I realize that I should be working on my essay for AP English. "Compare the tone and/or mood in two of the poems listed below." I choose "Elegy Written in a Country Churchyard" by Thomas Gray and a part of "The Dunciad" by Alexander Pope. We had read both of the 18th-century poems recently, and I could immediately see the contrast in tone and mood. By the time I finish a rough draft of the paper, it is after 11 o'clock. I go quietly back downstairs, thinking Mom might be in bed, but she is still up. Dad has already gone to bed.

"Would you read over my paper for AP English sometime before tomorrow night and see if it makes sense?" I ask. I have learned that it is not a good idea to ask Mom to read my work at the last minute.

"Sure," she says. "So, you don't want to go to prom at all? Is Sophie going?"

"Yeah, Sophie's going with Jason, but no one has asked me, and I'm not sure whether I want to go unless I have a date."

"Well, I understand, but I did hear some girls today saying that they are going together, so you do have options. You probably need to think about a dress if you decide to go."

"I know. Juan is going to ask Grace, I think."

"Really? Today, I heard her talking with the girls who are going as a group. So, apparently he has not asked her yet. What about Bert? Maybe he'll ask you," suggests Mom.

"I doubt it. Sophie says Todd will ask me, but I don't think so."

"We'll see. Either one would be lucky to have you as a prom date. That's all I can say."

"Thank you, Mom."

When I return to my room, I think about Bert. Since he moved here last year and became Juan's debating partner, I've gotten to know him fairly well. He wants to be a diplomat, and he probably will be. He says the U.S. could do a lot more in relating to other countries. His mom and dad travel a lot, and he has been out of the country several times. His dad works with some tech company as its legal counsel. Bert seems to know a lot about other cultures. He also has a lot of sympathy for immigrants who come from South America and other places. Most of the people around here have a very narrow view of things, and sometimes I think he doesn't relate well to them. But I like him, and he and Juan get along well, too.

CHAPTER 18

Tomorrow is the day for the Juan Garcia Cup, a faculty vs. student soccer game. Juan coaches the student team each year as they battle the teachers for a trophy he has designed. Last year the proceeds went to help Juan do some things on his wish list, but this year Juan insists that it fund a scholarship for another student who has overcome a difficult challenge. The soccer coach organized the event to underscore the school's support for Juan as he continues his drawn-out battle with cancer, and it's a big event.

All of Juan's friends meet right after school to help get ready for the soccer game to start at 4 o'clock. I help with ticket sales, Bert and Todd are playing in the game, and some of the others either help with tickets or in the concession booth.

Juan is so excited. Coach Miller plays on the teachers' team and coaches too, and he and Juan are kidding back and forth about who will win. I'm not sure if the teachers have just let the students win the last two years, or whether the students were better, but that's the way it has gone.

The spirit is always good because everyone knows they're doing it all for Juan. This time it is especially significant because it could be Juan's last time to be a part of the event personally. I'm not sure if all students are aware that he was told last spring that he had only three to six months to live, but I'm sure most of them do. All of us are cheering the student team on in a bittersweet kind of way.

It's a close game, but when it's over, it's another 2–1 win for Juan and his student team. Bert leads the team as they march by for a "high-five" from Juan.

When it's time for Juan to accept the cup for his team, he has a big smile on his face. Coach Miller makes the official presentation and congratulates Juan on his coaching the students to victory.

Leading up to the soccer event, I had been so busy helping Juan and the others get ready for it that I had not thought much about prom, but now that it's behind us, I am thinking about who's going with whom, and how I feel about going.

I have been wondering if Juan has asked Grace to go to the prom with him yet. When I see him in the hallway, I ask him if he plans to ask her. He says he does but that he needs some help. Later that day I ask him if he wants to come to my house after school and tell me what he needs.

When Juan gets to my house, he asks if we have any poster board. We do—teachers always have poster board. I bring him a marker, and he prints in large letters: "Betty doesn't want to third-wheel this time. Will you walk to prom with me?" I can't remember when we started calling his wheelchair Betty, or who came up with the idea. All I know is that for a long time we've all called it Betty. When Juan finishes, he tells me he wants to show the poster to Grace the next morning in the hall in front of the office, and he needs me to come to the office with her and see him give her the invitation.

I am in homeroom with Grace, so when she gets called to the office, I ask the teacher if I can go with her, and she lets me. Grace thinks she is in trouble.

When we approach the office door and it starts to open, Grace steps aside because she doesn't know who is coming out. Juan has the poster perched on his feet. When she sees Juan, she smiles but doesn't look at the poster at all. "What are you doing here?" she asks. He grabs the poster and holds it up.

"Calling you to the office—you're in trouble, big trouble."

"What…?" Grace looks at the poster and realizes what he is doing.

She gets this big grin on her face. "Well… yes, I'll go with you to the prom!" We all have a big laugh, and the principal walks out, smiles at Juan and Grace and tells us it's time to get back to class.

In my AP English class, some girls ask me to go with their group of five or six to the prom. I give consideration to their invitation, so on Saturday morning I tell Mom that I want to look for a prom dress—just in case I get invited or decide to go with the girls. We don't find a dress on our shopping trip, but I'm okay with that because the prom is still three weeks away.

CHAPTER 19

I am excited about celebrating with the debate team. When we are gathered at Eddie's, the talk quickly turns to prom plans. Everyone knows about Juan's dramatic invitation to Grace, and then Jason says, "Sophie and I are going to the prom together, aren't we Sophie?" Sophie raises her eyebrows. She doesn't seem too excited about it, but nods her head. It doesn't seem like her to act that way, but who knows?

"Really?" asks Bert. "Why don't we all go eat together and then go to my house afterward—provided my parents will let us."

"Who are you taking to the prom, Bert?" asks Juan.

"I've asked this girl who goes to Cherokee County High. I think she'll go with me."

Sophie looks around the table. "So, I guess that leaves Alice and Todd. Are you all going together?"

Todd looks at me. I can feel the heat rising from my neck all the way up to my hairline. I can't think of anything clever to say. I want to sink down through my chair. As usual, Todd rescues me.

"Look, I'd love to go to the prom with Alice, but I'm sure she's got to decide about other invitations before she can accept mine. We'll let you know later about who we're going with. Won't we, Alice?" I nod, thankful for his words.

"Okay, but what about going to eat with the team? Do you want to do that?" asks Bert.

We all agree that we think it's a good idea, and Bert says he'll see if his mom will let us come to their house afterwards. After the talk about prom, we all settle into tonight's celebration of the end of our high school debate experience. Even though I'm still not the confident person I'd like to be, I realize that I've grown a lot in my ability to enjoy being a part of this group of friends.

Mom said she would stay home and get things ready for having dessert and watching the movie, *The Great Debaters*. I send her a text when we leave Eddie's. My fudge cake is sitting on the kitchen counter when we get there. I'm proud that I know how to make it, because it is a favorite with everyone, especially Jason and Juan. They are addicted to chocolate, I think. By the time all the debaters add their snacks, we decide we may not have needed to go to Eddie's for dinner.

"What's the movie about?" inquires Sophie. "I know it's about debaters, but what's the plot?"

"It's based on a true story from the 1930s," answers Mom. "It was produced in 2007 and stars Denzel Washington. One of the producers was Oprah Winfrey."

"Yeah," says Bert. "It's about this professor at a historically Black college who starts a debate team, and they end up beating some big university—Harvard, I think."

"At that time, it was unheard of for a predominately Black college to even have a debate team," notes Mom. "Now it wouldn't be a big deal, but it was then."

It was fascinating to watch. Bert was the only one of us who had seen it, but he enjoyed it again. Todd especially liked it since he loves history.

"Are any of you planning to debate in college?" Mom asks when the movie is finished.

"I hope to," says Bert. "I guess it depends on where I go. I haven't decided yet for sure."

"It's the same way with me," says Todd. "I'm hoping to get a basketball scholarship, and if I do, I may have a problem with time to debate. I would love to. I love history, and debating has been one of my favorite activities in high school—even more than basketball."

"That's my situation," says Sophie. "If I get a basketball scholarship, I may not have time to debate."

"Where are you going to college?" Mom asks her.

"I'm not sure. Coach Callahan is recommending me for a basketball scholarship at the college he went to in Ohio," she says.

"Great. I hope that works out for you."

"Do you know what you want to major in?" asks Dad. "You might want to think about that, too."

"Not really. I would like to do social work maybe, but I haven't really thought about it much."

"I understand that. You have a lot of choices. You might want to look at all the majors in the college you choose, and see what they have in that general area. You can narrow it down later."

"What about you, Todd?" asks Dad.

"I want to be a teacher, like Mrs. Jarvis. Except I'll teach history," Todd says, looking at Mom. "Do you recommend that, Mrs. Jarvis?"

Mom smiles. "Yes and no. If you really like teaching, it's a great profession. If you go into it thinking you'll make a lot of money, or that it's an easy job, then it's probably not a good choice. Me—I love it. I love working with students, and

I see a lot of promise in the younger generation. But it's a job that demands a lot of work both inside and outside the classroom, and you don't get a lot of rewards."

I don't want the discussion to get to what I want to do, because I don't know, so I change the subject. I go to the kitchen counter and look at all the food. "What are we going to do with all this food?" I ask. "You guys need to take what you brought home with you, and if any of you want to take a piece of cake, you can do that."

"I definitely want a piece," says Bert.

"Me too," adds Juan.

Juan is looking a little pale lately, and I notice that he isn't talking as much as usual. I watch him as he cuts a piece of cake and wraps it in the foil I lay out on the counter. The counter is a little high for him in his wheelchair, but he manages to get it without help. When he finishes wrapping his cake and moves away, Bert steps in to get his.

I am standing at the sink pouring out leftover drinks when Todd steps in beside me and says casually, "I hope they didn't embarrass you by talking about us going to the prom together, but would you actually consider going with me? I really hope you will."

I look up at him and see a genuine smile. I swallow hard. "Yes, I'd love to."

I never noticed that Todd has a dimple on the right side of his face until that smile. A blush rushes to my cheeks and neck as we continue to look at each other. Despite my obvious tell, I don't feel embarrassed in front of him at all. It is hard not to notice how attractive he is. I never allowed myself to think about him in that way until now.

After a few seconds of awkward tension, Todd moves back to where the rest of the students are packing up the food they'd brought or getting a piece of cake to take home.

Soon they all begin to leave. Everyone seems a little hesitant, and I hate to see them go. We tell each other we've enjoyed debating together, and wish each other well in the coming year. We agree to keep one another informed as we make decisions about college. Although Juan says he's going to the local community college, we all know that his main goal is to graduate from high school. He was put on hospice care a few months ago, but so far he has been able to be up and about, going with us to baseball and soccer games and other school activities.

CHAPTER 20

This Saturday morning, I am both excited and anxious when I awake. I look over at my prom dress hanging on the back of my closet door. It's tonight! The sun is shining through the window, and I can see the sequined bodice of the powder-blue dress. It was my favorite of the ones at the boutique. I think it cost more than Mom had planned to pay, but when I said it was my favorite, she didn't seem to mind. The heels are almost the exact color of the dress.

While lying in bed, I imagine myself dancing in the decorated hall where the prom will be. The juniors have chosen the theme, "Night of Dreams," and they are decorating with our school colors. I remember helping with decorations last year, and I think I probably enjoyed last year more than I will this year. I didn't have to dress up and impress anyone.

My friends are all meeting at our house at 4:30 this afternoon before we go to eat. Dad said he will take our pictures while we are dressed up. I remember that Mom has to do something this morning—I can't remember what, but I am supposed to get up and start getting the house cleaned. I put on a robe and go downstairs where my dad is reading the newspaper and listening to the news on television.

"When will Mom be home?" I ask.

"It's probably going to be around noon, I think." Dad looks up. "Aren't you supposed to clean house for her since your friends are coming over?"

"Yeah, I know. I'll get started in a while. Right now, I'm going to eat some cereal."

"How many of your friends are coming to get pictures made?"

"It's just the debate team. We're all going together. I guess there'll be two extras: Grace is going with Juan, and Bert is bringing a girl who doesn't go to our school."

"So, there'll be eight?"

"Yes, I think that's all. Why don't you make some group pictures, and then a picture of each couple. Oh, and make some pictures of all the girls and some of all the boys."

"I can do that." Dad is an amateur photographer. He loves fooling around with a camera. He has all these different lenses, and most of his pictures turn out as well as most of the ones taken by professional photographers. Plus, it's less expensive for all of us because he doesn't charge for his "time and talent" as he says.

By the time Mom gets home, I have completed the "To Do" list she left on the table. It will soon be time to start getting ready for the prom. Ms. Lucas comes over at 1 o'clock to fix my hair. When she finishes, I look beautiful. Then I put on my dress and shoes, and Mom helps me with my make-up. Dad is snapping pictures. He even takes one of Mom putting on my blush. I am ready before my friends come, so Dad takes a few pictures of me by myself and one with Mom. Then Mom takes a picture of me with Dad.

My friends begin showing up early for group pictures. Todd brings me flowers that look beautiful with the color of my dress. He had me text him a picture of the dress yesterday, so he could give it to the florist. It takes us a few minutes to locate the best place for pictures, but since it's a beautiful spring day, we decide that our back lawn will be the prettiest. Mom has a little flower garden out there, and several flowers are in bloom. All the shrubs provide a beautiful green background. We have our group picture taken, and then each couple decides where they want to have their picture made. Bert's mother made a reservation for us at 6:30 at Longhorn's. She said they don't normally make reservations, but for this special occasion, they did. (Bert's mother knows the manager.)

When we arrive at the restaurant, Bert and Todd help Juan with his wheelchair while the rest of us go on in. Jason seems about as uncomfortable in this social situation as I do. Fortunately, both Todd and Sophie are relaxed—or at least Todd is. Sophie is a little "unsettled," I think. I'm not sure what her problem is tonight. Maybe it's just because Jason is not good with a date. I watch her all during dinner, and she seems a little edgy. When Jason asks her a question about basketball, she snaps at him. And then when Todd says that most of the teachers will be at the prom tonight, Sophie is adamant that he is wrong, adding that Coach Callahan has said he is not coming.

"I didn't say that he was," said Todd. "I was just saying that most of the teachers would."

"Well, I just wanted you to know that not all of them would be," she said. I thought it strange that it would matter to her. Something just doesn't seem right to me about the relationship between Sophie and Coach Callahan, and the way she's acting tonight makes me suspect something even more.

By the time we leave the restaurant, I look forward to getting on the dance floor—just to avoid talking to one another. Todd is a good dancer, and he isn't particular about whether it's a slow or fast song or if I want to dance every number or sit one out. He's a good date for someone like me, I guess. During a break from dancing, I find a bench and sit down for a bit. Jason and Sophie "debate" about whether to dance every number. Bert's date only likes to dance the slow songs. Grace and Juan seem to be having a good time, dancing and laughing with friends. Juan seems to feel good tonight, which makes me happy. I know he can't be really comfortable with his prosthetic, because he hates it, but he's determined.

Bert's mom has invited all of us to their house for a while, but says we can only stay until 1 a.m. She has invited some of Bert's other friends in addition to our group. The prom is over at 11:00, so we'll have nearly two hours there. That's fine with me. When we arrive, she has finger foods and soft drinks set up on the patio and music playing. Some of the songs are the same ones the D.J. played at prom, and some of the kids start dancing to the music.

I have always known that Bert's dad traveled a lot and that they have lived in several different places. In debate, I learned that Bert has been in school in several different states and in at least one foreign country—Lebanon, I think. I have never thought much about the impact that would make on him, though.

After we've been there a while, Bert's mother stops the music, and tells us that she and Bert's dad have an announcement to make.

"First, I want to thank all of you for coming over," she says. "Bert really has enjoyed getting to know you. I think this is the first time he has really felt a part of a class. Since we move around so much, it's often been hard for him to make friends, but he's really enjoyed all of you. Thank you for that. Now, Bert's dad has an announcement."

Bert's dad stands up and says, "Well, we're doing it again. I have been assigned to a new location out in California. Bert can tell you of his college plans, but we'll be moving in July, and we thought you should know." I guess Bert refused to participate in these little family speeches, because he had mysteriously disappeared when his dad sat down.

As soon as Bert returned, Sophie approached him. "Where are you going to college? Somewhere in California, I'll bet."

"Actually, no. I was accepted to George Washington University in D.C. before Dad knew he would be going to Los Angeles."

"Are your parents okay with you being so far away from them?"

Bert looks over at his mother. "Not really, but they understand that if I'm going to be a diplomat, I need to be located where I can get the right kind of experience and observation."

Sophie and Jason rode over to Bert's with Todd and me, so after the party we drop them off at school so Jason can get his car. This is when I get a little nervous. Will Todd try to kiss me goodnight? If he does, should I let him? I imagine all sorts of scenarios as we drive home.

"Are you okay?" he asks as we pull in our driveway. "You haven't said a word since we left the school."

"I'm okay. I just don't know how to act in this situation."

"What do you mean?"

"Well, this is a lot different from debate." I shift in the car seat. "Do you date a lot?"

"No. I've gone to the movies with a girl a few times, but I don't date much. I don't have time for it."

"Me either."

"I've really had fun going to the prom with you, Alice. You're a good dancer. It's been a good evening."

We are in front of our house, and Todd parks the car. "I'll walk you to the door."

I sit dutifully inside until he comes around and opens my car door. Then we walk side by side up to my door.

"Thank you for going with me," Todd tells me. "It's been great." Then he cups my chin in his hand and gives me a quick kiss on the lips. "See you Monday," he says as he runs back down the sidewalk. I stand there for a few moments. Now, that wasn't so bad, was it?

When I walk in, I don't see anyone. I go on into the kitchen where Mom is standing at the counter looking at the newspaper. Looking up, she says, "How was prom night?"

"Great. We really had a good time." And I meant it.

CHAPTER 21

Before graduation, students and teachers at Closeville High School come together to vote for the "Teacher of the Year." The person with the most votes is then eligible for the district-wide distinction. Closeville's Teacher of the Year will be announced in assembly today. We all have our favorites. I always hope Mom will be chosen but, so far, she hasn't been. We're all trying to guess who the winner is this year. Juan thinks it will be our Spanish teacher. Sophie says she hopes it's Mrs. Jarvis (Mom). And Todd says he thinks it'll be Coach Callahan.

"Your attention please," calls the principal. "We come here today to honor our Teacher of the Year. All of you voted for your choice last month. After tallying the votes, we are excited to announce that Coach Wade Callahan has been chosen as our Teacher of the Year. Come up here, Coach." The students begin to clap and cheer as he walks to the stage. "I want to ask our counselor, Ms. Willoughby, to read the recommendation from our school to the system."

Ms. Willoughby goes to the microphone and reads: "Closeville High School nominates Coach Wade Callahan for Teacher of the Year as our system representative. Coach Callahan has made an astonishing contribution to our school this year. For the first time in decades our girls' basketball team has won the region championship and had the opportunity to compete at the state level. Secondly, the coach has 'made history' with his history classes. His students have scored higher on standardized tests than they have in years. He encourages students both on the basketball court and in the classroom. Congratulations, Coach Callahan!"

Both students and teachers give him a standing ovation as they're clapping and cheering. I stand and clap too. I see both Juan and Sophie cheering wildly, and Mom is cheering, too. But I have mixed feelings. Coach Callahan takes the mic and thanks both students and teachers for the honor of representing CHS in this way.

After that, I push all the feelings I've had about him to the back of my mind. Obviously, I am the one who is wrong. All my friends, along with the teachers, parents, and community leaders seem to think he is a wonderful person. He is given a commendation by the Rotary Club that holds its monthly meetings at our school.

A week later we have our annual awards day at school, and Sophie and I are seated with the other seniors. To save time, the principal just calls out names of the students having high grade-point averages, but for other recognitions students come to the platform. Juan gets to present the new scholarship award that is given in his honor. Grace and I help him up the ramp to the stage, and he waits with the others until he is given the microphone to make his presentation. A hush falls over the crowd when he begins to speak.

"When the opportunity arose for this scholarship, I decided to call it the Warrior Award. I wanted the person who receives it to be someone who has faced a challenge and overcome it. Courage, above all things, is the first quality of a warrior. When faced with adversity, you can choose to give up, or you can choose to overcome the obstacle.

"Five years ago, I was faced with my first challenge: a tumor in my leg. Throughout these last five years, I have had other challenges, but with each one, I have tried to face them with courage and a smile. I have come to realize that bad things happen in life, but it is how you respond to them that defines your character.

"This award is presented to a person who has faced challenges for the last few years and yet is overcoming everything with class, and I know she will achieve all of her goals in life. The first annual Warrior Award goes to Mandy Craft."

There is wild cheering as Mandy approaches the stage. Although many students do not know the details of Mandy's problems, most of the seniors know that she was abused by some relative—an uncle, I think—and finally showed much bravery and courage by coming forward and telling what had happened to her in order to save her little sisters from the same fate. Even after all her struggles, through counseling she has risen to the top of our class and is salutatorian this year. She is very deserving.

The principal calls Ms. Willoughby to the stage to make the next presentation. She takes the microphone and begins to talk. "Thank you. This is not one of our regular awards, but I think all of you should know about it. It came to me in the mail a few weeks ago. I am always amazed at the talent in our school. It is not often that talent in writing is recognized at the national level."

My ears perk up a little. She continues, "At this time, I would like to ask Alice Jarvis to come to the stage."

I freeze for a moment and then get up and move forward toward Ms. Willoughby as the audience starts applauding.

"Alice has won first place in a national contest for a short story she wrote last summer. It comes with a monetary award of $1,000."

As I approach the stage, Ms. Willoughby is sharing the name of the contest, the name of my story, and why they chose me. At the moment I can't even think. All I know is that suddenly I am a little more confident as I walk up on the stage amidst applause and shouts of congratulations. Ms. Willoughby gives me a hug and hands me the papers. Fortunately, she does not ask me to speak, but she does put her arm around me and points toward Mom, who is standing in front of the stage trying to get a picture of us.

Maybe this is the beginning of a different version of Alice. Maybe there is something valuable in me, even though I never know what to say or how to say what I do know.

"What will you do with all that money?" someone asks as I go back to my seat.

"I have no idea right now," I respond.

"I can help you spend it," another voice offers.

We are moving out of the auditorium now, going back to class, but I keep thinking about the certificate and check that Ms. Willoughby has given me for my short story. I still can't believe I actually won. I thought, or hoped, I might place third or fourth, or get honorable mention, but I never expected to be the winner.

After school I go by Mom's classroom. When I walk in, several students are finishing a meeting with her. As soon as they leave, she says, "Well, congratulations, girl! I didn't know we were going to have a celebrity in our house. I just called your dad a few minutes ago and told him. I guess we'll have to go out tonight and celebrate. Be thinking of where you want to eat dinner."

"Thanks, Mom. You didn't know I had submitted that story, did you? I wanted to do it all by myself with no help from anyone."

"You did, and you won. You have every right to be proud of yourself. I've always known you have much more talent and ability than you think. I'm glad somebody else recognized it too."

Chapter 22

I rode to school with Mom today because I had to leave my car at the shop late yesterday to get it serviced. Mom said she'd need to stay late to work with some students, so I decide to stop by the library to look up some stuff for my art class.

As I am about to enter the library, Todd is coming up the hall and we stop to talk. After chatting a little about our graduation and college plans, I ask him if Juan was at Callahan's house the day before. He says, "I don't think so. Most of us haven't been going since Mrs. Callahan left."

"What do you mean?... Like, left the coach?"

"I don't know much about it. We were over there one night, and someone asked what time she would be coming home. He was walking through the living room and he said, 'she won't' and walked on into the kitchen. We looked at each other and shrugged. Later someone at school said she had left him."

"So, none of you go over there anymore?"

"I think a few of them still go. I'm not sure."

"Does Sophie still go over there?" I ask.

"She may. I'm not sure who does. I haven't been over there in a few weeks, but I'm pretty sure Juan hasn't been since I quit going."

It suddenly hits me that I haven't talked to Sophie much lately. I remember that Sophie did not talk much to me at the last debate tournament, and that although we talked at the party that night, she had not mentioned anything about going to Coach Callahan's. Before the last tournament she was talking a lot about going to the Coach's house.

"Why did you stop going over there?"

Todd hesitates. "I don't know. I know this is going to sound strange, but I just didn't want to go any more."

My stomach feels like it is in a knot. I feel sick.

I knew, even back when she called him "Wade" by accident, that Sophie's friendship with Coach Callahan was something different than a student-teacher relationship should be, but I tried not to admit it, partly because I didn't know what to do about it, and partly because I did know. When you're as shy as I am, you always try to find a way not to confront people about things that make you uncomfortable. I have practiced that skill ever since I can remember. There have been so many times when it would have been much easier for me if I had just told someone something, but I didn't. Like the time I was sick at my stomach in the 2nd grade, and I just kept pretending I was okay until I threw up all over the floor of my classroom. And the time I forgot my lunch and knew my teacher would have given me lunch money because she knew Mom, but I just didn't eat all day. So now I've refused to deal with the problem with Sophie until I can't deny it any longer, and I have to say something to her, even if it blows up in my face.

Chapter 23

Our senior year is winding down. Most of my friends are beginning to hear from colleges where they have applied. When Isabella tells me that she has been accepted at Case Western, her first choice, I want to be happy for her. So much has been going on that I have not had time to think much about my own applications, though. At the same time, her announcement reminds me that I still have not heard from Auburn. When I'd been accepted by the other colleges I'd applied to, Mom said I could wait a few weeks to respond until I heard from Auburn. But now I'm getting worried, thinking that maybe I won't be accepted there. As usual, I am thinking the worst. Todd told me last week that he has been accepted by Toccoa Falls College to play basketball. Of course, I don't know what is going to happen with Sophie. I can't imagine her going off to Ohio, but she may.

It's Friday, and I'm very annoyed with everything as I drive home. Nothing has gone right the whole day. I got my American Literature paper back, with red ink splattered all over it telling me what I had done wrong, or what I could do to make it better. What is the purpose of making it better when I am going to throw it in the trash can when I get home?

As I'm turning into my driveway, I realize I don't have my house key with me. There is a circular driveway in front of our house, so I just turn around and head back to school.

"I thought you'd already left," says Mom when I walk into her room.

"I had, but I didn't have a key. Can I borrow yours?"

"May I…" That's the price of being an English teacher's daughter.

"Whatever."

She hands me her key, and I head back home. After parking the car, I remember that no one has been home since the mail has come, so I decide to take it in. Usually, it's mostly junk mail. Sometimes Mom will call out, "Current Resident, is that you, Alice? You do still live here, don't you?"

I walk to the mailbox, almost dropping my notebook and books because I am distracted by the next-door neighbor's dog barking at me. When I open the mailbox, I find only one letter—hardly worth the effort to walk down the driveway. I shift my books a little to get a free hand to reach in and pick it up. I see "Alice

Jarvis" on the front of the envelope. Then I look at the return address: "Auburn University."

I almost drop my books, but I run back up the driveway and manage to get the key out of my pocket and open the door. Within seconds, I am twirling around the living room informing my imaginary listeners that I have been accepted to Auburn.

As soon as I calm down, I call Mom and tell her. Her enthusiasm isn't quite as great as mine, but I can tell she is happy for me. Then I text Juan. I think about telling Sophie, but decide to wait.

CHAPTER 24

It's Sunday afternoon and I've asked Sophie to come over a while. Dad is at the golf course, and Mom is at the school working on plans for her next teaching unit. Since they are not at home, Sophie and I are sitting in our den with the television on, but not really watching or listening to it. We are talking about graduation, college, and other stuff. When she mentions something about the scholarship Coach Callahan has recommended her for, I see my opening.

"Sophie, I asked you to come over because I want to talk to you."

"Why?"

"I have been concerned for some time about you and Coach Callahan. You go over there a lot, even since Mrs. Callahan left, and you talk about him almost like he's your boyfriend instead of your basketball coach. What is going on?"

When she says nothing, I continue. "Teachers aren't supposed to have that kind of relationship with their students. I overheard Mom talk about it once, and she mentioned that teachers have gotten fired for that sort of thing. It's also against the law, I think. So, if someone finds out about you and Coach Callahan, they would have to report it and he could get arrested.

When I finish confronting her with my suspicions, Sophie stiffens in her chair. Her face is red, and she reaches for her purse on the floor and draws it close to her side. I think for a moment she is going to leave, but she doesn't. It's the quietest I've ever seen her. She glances downward for what seems like a long time, breathing slowly. Finally, she takes a deep breath and says, "I don't know what you're talking about."

"You don't?" The air hangs between us, thick and tangible.

"What are you trying to suggest?" Before I can answer, she adds, "You're just trying to make me look bad. Who have you told about this?"

"No one. I wouldn't do that."

"Well! I'm glad, but if anyone says anything, I'll know you are lying to me. And if I find out that you're talking about me behind my back, I'll never speak to you again."

"I'm sorry if my concerns hurt you, Sophie. Of course, I won't tell anyone right now, but what you're doing is very serious. I don't blame you; I blame Coach Callahan."

"Well, if it's such a big deal to you, I won't go over there so much, but you'd better not start blabbing about it to anyone else. It's really not any of your business." She grabs her purse and heads for the door.

"Sophie, I'm only saying these things because you are my friend and I'm concerned."

Sophie slams the door as she walks out toward her car. I walk upstairs and fall onto my bed and cry for a long time before falling asleep. The next thing I know, Mom is shaking me.

"Alice, are you alright?" she asks.

"Yes. I was just taking a nap. What time is it?"

"It's 6 o'clock. I thought you said Sophie was coming over."

"She did, but she didn't stay long. Her mother wanted her to come home," I lie. "I decided to take a nap. I'll be down in a minute."

I don't say anything to Mom about Sophie because I know what she'd do. She would probably be required to report the coach. I want to think about what I should do, who I can talk to. I can't talk to Juan right now because he has enough problems of his own. I feel sick again as I remember Sophie's angry words about not telling anyone and her slamming of the door. Am I really right in believing all these things about our "teacher of the year"?

As I think of people who might help me decide what to do, Grace comes to my mind. She always seems so calm. She probably wouldn't actually tell me what to do, but she might help me in some way. Before I go downstairs, I text her and ask if I can talk to her after school tomorrow.

"Sure. Can I just come by your house right after school?"

I text her right back. "That's perfect."

When I go downstairs, I feel a little bad about not telling Mom about what's going on with Sophie, but I feel like I have to handle this myself. It sure is a lot easier just to let my parents help with everything, but maybe I need to start doing more things on my own.

All day Monday I keep thinking of what I need to say to Grace when I meet with her this afternoon. She has probably been at the Callahans' a lot more than I have, so she may know more than I do about what goes on. I wonder if she still goes over there. She probably doesn't since Todd and Juan don't seem to be going. What if she doesn't think anything is wrong? What will I do then?

As soon as school is out, I run by Mom's room and then head home. I have only been there about 10 minutes when Grace arrives. I greet her at the door.

"Are you okay? Is anything wrong? I was surprised that you wanted to talk to me."

I hesitate a moment, as usual. "I want to talk to you about Sophie."

"Oh." Her look tells me that she may have some awareness of what I'm going to say, but she keeps quiet for a few moments. She seems to be waiting for me to continue.

"I'm concerned about her."

"What are you concerned about?"

I finally just plunge in. "I think she spends too much time with Coach Callahan, and I think he …" I don't know how to put it.

"You think he's abusing her?"

"Yes, I do." I've finally said it to someone—out loud. I breathe a sigh of relief.

Grace sits there a moment, with a questioning look on her face. She doesn't say I'm wrong, but she doesn't confirm anything either. She just sits there.

Finally, she asks, "What makes you think that?" Her blond curls make her face look angelic.

I tell her about Sophie's comments and the fact that she keeps going over to Coach Callahan's house even though his wife has left him and most of the other students have stopped going. I also tell her about the scholarship he is supposedly getting for her.

"That might explain some of the things the guys have said over the last few weeks," Grace says.

"I wanted to talk to you because I'm sure you know the Callahans a lot better than I do and have been at their house much more than I have."

"Well, actually that's not true. I know you and I were there the same night, but that's one of the few times I have been there. I have not been at all this year."

"Oh, I guess I just assumed you came all the time. By the way, what did you mean by 'that might explain some of the things the guys have said'? Did you mean Todd and Juan?"

"I just remember Todd saying he couldn't believe Sophie is still going over there, and Juan said maybe she likes it better since Mrs. Callahan left. But I didn't know who he was talking about, or even that they were talking about going to the coach's. In fact, I didn't even know that his wife had left him until you just told me."

"I confronted Sophie yesterday, and she got really mad and denied it all. But Grace, I just can't ignore this. I've got to tell someone. What should I do?"

"I can't tell you what to do, Alice, but I think Sophie should be thankful she has a friend like you, who is concerned enough to intervene in the situation."

"But what if I'm wrong? What if he really isn't abusing her? Won't I look like a fool?"

Grace looks me straight in the eye. "Maybe. It's a risk you have to decide if it's worth taking. What do you plan to do?"

"I don't know. I want to help Sophie, but she doesn't seem to want my help. She got so mad and walked out of my house. She acted like I was her enemy."

"Well, I can't tell you what to do, but I do know that sometimes doing the right thing doesn't make everyone happy."

"I appreciate your listening, and please don't say anything to anyone about this. I'll just have to decide what to do. But it has helped to talk to you."

When Grace leaves, I know what I have to do. My stomach is churning as she backs out of my driveway. I want to call to her for help, but I know I can't. This is my problem, and I'll have to deal with it.

CHAPTER 25

Tuesday morning, I go by Ms. Willoughby's office and ask if I can talk with her during lunch. She says yes, of course. I'm sure she thinks I'm coming to talk about my college applications. At noon she is ready for me and has all my paperwork about colleges on her desk.

"Ms. Willoughby, I'm not here about college. I want to talk to you about something else."

"Oh? What is it, dear?" I'm sure all the tension in my body shows in my face.

I don't know where to start, so I just blurt it out. "I'm worried about Sophie and Coach Callahan."

"What do you mean?"

"I'm pretty sure Sophie is spending too much time with Coach Callahan, especially since his wife left him."

"His wife has left him?" Ms. Willoughby seems shocked.

"I just learned that last week." Then I pour out the whole story. "Several students had been going over there on Monday nights for a long time. Last year, I went with Sophie one night, but I didn't really enjoy it. I just didn't feel comfortable around him, but you know I'm not very outgoing, so I just thought it was me. Todd and Juan seemed to like going there. Several of the girls on the basketball team were there."

Ms. Willoughby looks at me. "Did you suspect anything then?"

"Not exactly. I just felt uncomfortable." I hesitated. "Something made me want Juan and Sophie, especially Sophie, not to go there, but I couldn't figure out why. That was when I asked Mom if our debate team could come to our house on Monday nights. We did for the rest of the year. But when this year began, I kind of forgot about it."

"Did the rest of the kids go back to the Coach's on Mondays?"

"I guess, at least Sophie, Todd, and Juan did. Bert and Jason never went I don't think."

Ms. Willoughby gets up and paces around. "Did you ever ask Sophie about what she thinks about the coach?"

"Once I asked her if she felt comfortable going over there. She acted kind of mad and said I was uncomfortable with everybody. Later she apologized for blowing up at me."

"What else has made you concerned?"

"Well, at one of our debate tournaments Sophie started to tell me that Coach Callahan had recommended her for a basketball scholarship. Anyway, she called him 'Wade' and then corrected herself. That just seemed odd, and it didn't seem right. But then later when he got all those awards, and everyone seemed to like him so well, I just thought I must be wrong."

Ms. Willoughby nods. "And what made you finally decide to come here and tell me, Alice?"

"It started when I asked Todd if Juan had been at Coach Callahan's on Monday night. He said he didn't think so, because most of the kids had not been going over there since Mrs. Callahan had left. Of course, I didn't know she had left. He went on to say that maybe Sophie still goes over there. I remembered hearing Sophie talk as if she might be going more than just on Mondays. That's when I had to admit that something was going on. I really didn't want to admit it, or confront Sophie, because, well, you know how I am."

"So, you just came to me?"

"Well, no. I thought I owed it to Sophie to confront her first. I asked her to come over Sunday. I told her all I had noticed. Of course, she denied that anything was going on, and then got mad and left. That's when I decided to come to you."

"Good for you, Alice. You've done the right thing. Did you tell your mother?"

"No. I'm trying to grow up and handle things myself. I don't object if you think Mom should know, but I don't want it to be her problem."

"I understand. Alice, I will look into this and will probably have to report it to the authorities. Are you aware that you might have to testify if it should go to court?"

I nod my head yes.

"It could get ugly. A lot of parents, teachers, and other people in our community really like Coach Callahan. They will not take kindly to any negative stories about him."

"I know." But I really have no idea.

"It may be a few weeks before I will have any feedback for you, but I will look into it. And don't say anything else to Sophie about it. If she should happen to decide to be honest with you about what's going on, though, let me know, and I will help in any way I can."

I am glad I talked to Ms. Willoughby for two reasons. One is that she knows what to do, and the other is that I did it without help. Now I can confide in Mom, but she will not have to be responsible for reporting the alleged abuse. It makes me feel like I am making progress in dealing with things on my own. I go back to class feeling a little more confident in myself.

That night when Mom gets home from school and we are eating dinner, I tell her about all that has happened and my meeting with Ms. Willoughby. I can tell she is upset, but she says that I've done the right thing. Later, when Dad gets home, we both tell him.

"Things could get bad, according to Ms. Willoughby," says Mom. "You know, Coach Callahan is really liked by everyone. He got Teacher of the Year and that civic club award. Even Todd is crazy about him. But he and Juan have quit going to the coach's house. Why, I'm not sure. They might know something. I'm afraid to say anything to anyone."

CHAPTER 26

One week after confiding in Ms. Willoughby, I am called back into her office. My stomach tightens with nervous energy as I make my way there. As I enter, I see Mom sitting there. I just plop down in a chair and don't say a word.

Ms. Willoughby tells us: "I asked the two of you to come in here first, because I have some news, and I'm afraid you may not have a good day because of it. After I spoke to you last week, I talked to a friend of mine on the police force. He immediately started asking questions, and has learned that there is certainly some truth to what you say, Alice. As of today, Coach Callahan will not be allowed in the school." I swallow hard.

"What's the next step? Where will law enforcement go from here?" Mom asks.

"They will continue to look into it. He won't be arrested until the investigation is finished. The problem is that he has so many supporters in the school and community. Several people are really upset. I have not given anyone your name, but it's only a matter of time before someone figures it out. It probably was not good for me to have you come in here this morning, but I thought you should know what is taking place. For today, just pretend you don't know anything."

As we walk out of Ms. Willoughby's office, I look around to see if anyone seems to notice us. I don't see any people looking our way. Mom goes to her classroom, and I go to my homeroom. All morning I am aware of anyone who gives any particular attention to me. I see a substitute teacher in Coach Callahan's room. I decide that most students don't know why he is absent today. That makes me feel a little more at ease.

The next day when I enter the hallway where Mom's room is, I notice a group of students at the end of the hall. Todd is among them. As I get close, I hear him say, "Alice might know something." I catch my breath. Oh no.

"Alice," one of the girls says, "do you know why Coach Callahan has been suspended or something?"

I shake my head no. "I saw he had a sub yesterday. Is he not here today either?"

"Someone said he has been put on suspension for a week or so. They said something about an investigation," volunteers Todd.

I shrug my shoulders and head on down the hall. It's good that my response is typical of me. No one expects me to say anything, since I don't usually talk anyway. All day there is a growing tension, a swell of support for "the best teacher we have." I try to avoid discussions about Coach Callahan. I also try to avoid contact with Sophie. She and I don't have any classes together this semester, but she has the same lunch period. Today I try to get in line way ahead of her and get a seat where there will be no place close by for her to sit. I succeed, and as soon as I finish, I head for the library until time for my next class.

It is Thursday, and I am tired of trying to avoid Sophie. As I come out of the restroom after lunch, someone beside the door says "Boo!" I turn. It's Sophie.

"You sure have been avoiding me this week," she says.

"I thought you were mad at me."

She looks at me for a moment. "I know what you did," she says, then walks off quickly before I can answer. I'm afraid she will start telling others about what she thinks I've done, but I hear nothing to indicate she has throughout the day on Friday.

The next week, every time I see a group of students talking together, my heart stops. But still I get no indication that Sophie has said anything, and I have stopped trying to avoid her. One day after lunch as I'm walking down the hall, I hear someone call my name. I turn to see who it is.

"Alice, we want to talk to you," says a girl I barely know. I can't remember her name or where I've seen her. There are three other girls with her. At least one of them is on the girls' basketball team.

"What about?" I ask.

"We hear that you might have something to do with Coach Callahan's suspension," She waits for me to respond.

"What do you mean?" I ask. My heart is pounding. I know I should try to act calm.

"You shouldn't go around making accusations against good teachers. Coach Callahan is a really good teacher and coach, and he has done a lot for our basketball team."

"What makes you think I would do something like that?"

"Oh, I have my sources." I finally recognize her as a girl I saw at the coach's house the night I went there. I wonder if Sophie told her something.

Before I can say anything, the girls walk off laughing.

I go on to class and try to act normal the rest of the day. I don't want anyone to think I'm upset, but I feel almost sick at my stomach. How long will this go on, and who else will say things to me before this gets settled?

Time passes slowly. I hear nothing from Ms. Willoughby for weeks. I keep thinking the police will contact me, but they haven't. The good thing is that the other students seem to have lost interest. No one has said anything about Coach Callahan in a few days, and the substitute teacher is apparently carrying on with the last units in his history classes. I breathe a sigh of relief that no one has confronted me about the situation in a few days.

CHAPTER 27

After all that has happened, I assume Sophie is not going on the Cancun trip with us, and I haven't talked to her for a while. When Ms. Lucas needs our money for the trip, I don't try to ask Sophie about it. I told her I'd let her know when she needed to decide, but when the time comes, my courage fails me.

I am surprised when she sends me a text two weeks before graduation and asks if she can come over. I send her a response saying, "Of course. I'm home."

She is there in a short time. I see her pull in the driveway, and I notice that she walks slowly up the sidewalk with her head down. I wonder what this visit is about. I open the door, and when I see her face, I know that something is wrong. Is this about her parents? Jolene? Coach Callahan? At this point I realize that I may have been wrong not to try to reach out to her since that afternoon when she left angry.

"I don't know where to start," she begins.

"At the beginning?"

"I don't know where the beginning is anymore."

I wait. I listen for more. What does she need to say? I want to be encouraging.

"First, I guess I need to apologize for lying to you," she admits.

"About what?" I think I know the answer, though.

"About Coach Callahan. When I said I didn't know what you were talking about, I knew exactly what you were talking about. I wanted to think that I had found someone who cared for me, and that you were trying to mess it up. I didn't agree with you that it was his fault."

"What made you change your mind, or have you?" I ask.

"I have, but I still want to believe my fantasy. I've just had to confront reality."

She slumps on the couch, and beats the arm of it with her fist. "Why does everything have to be so complicated?" she shouts. "I wanted that stupid scholarship so much that I let him control my every move!"

"I'm not sure I understand what you mean."

"Well, you knew when you had me come over here that Mrs. Callahan had left him, didn't you?" I nod. "I was there when she left. She came in and found us sitting on the couch, and he had his arm around me. At that time, nothing had really happened between us, but it was pretty obvious that it was going in that direction. She screamed at him, ran in the bedroom, and packed a bag quickly and left."

"And after that?" I ask.

"You remember I told you he was recommending me for a basketball scholarship at the college he attended in Ohio?" I nod.

"After Mrs. Callahan left Coach, he kept insisting that I come over almost every day after school. And for a few weeks, it was pretty much like it was on the Monday that you were there—except on the other days it was just me. But then... then most of the gang didn't even come on Mondays. And then...things began to change when I'd go over. I don't even want to talk about it."

"You don't have to."

"Anyway, after I talked to you that day, I told him that it didn't look good for me to be coming over there all the time, and do you know what he said?" I shake my head. "He said if I wanted to get that scholarship, I'd be wise to spend time with him. That was when I realized I was in over my head. But what could I do? I needed the scholarship. I didn't know what to do, so I kept going."

"So, do you still go?"

"No. When he was suspended from his job, he thought I'd told on him. I hadn't, of course, but I only went back one time."

I look at my friend, and I wonder what went wrong. What could I have done? In the back of my mind, I have known since the first time I went to Coach Callahan's house last spring that she should not be going there. My instincts were right, but my pitiful efforts to help by having the debaters come to my house did nothing to stop things from happening. I have become a little braver now, but would I have done anything different if it had happened this spring? I don't know. I sit here absorbed in my own thoughts until Sophie breaks the silence.

"One reason I came here is to see if you will go to see Ms. Willoughby with me. She called me in today and asked if I would come and talk to her tomorrow before school. I think it has to do with Coach Callahan. I'm worried about what he may have told her." Sophie is twisting her purse strap around in her hands and biting her lip until they're almost bleeding.

"Of course, I'll go with you. Everything is going to be alright, Sophie. Nothing is your fault."

"Yes, it is." She begins to cry. "I should've known better. All I could think of was my own problems at home. He..." She stops for a moment. "I am so stupid. I actually thought he loved me!" She is crying hard now, and I move to sit beside her on the sofa and put my arm around her. I don't say anything, and we just sit there for several moments in silence, except for her crying.

"I'll be right with you tomorrow, Sophie. It doesn't really matter what the coach says about you. You aren't to blame."

"You are the best friend I have, Alice. I know I haven't always been kind to you, and I'm sorry."

"It's okay, we're okay. It'll all work out fine. It may not seem like it will, but it will."

Sophie has stopped crying now. "The other reason I wanted to come over is to see if I can still go on the senior trip to Cancun. Is it too late to be included?"

"I don't know, but I'll check."

"I am so ashamed. When you asked earlier, I just didn't want to leave Coach Callahan for that long. But now, I think it's the only way I can survive the next few weeks until the investigation is finished. I just want to be anywhere but in Closeville."

I call Ms. Lucas's number, and miraculously she answers on the first ring. "Hey, this is Alice."

"I know. What can I do for you, dear?" I can just see her grinning at me, knowing that her caller ID showed my name.

"I was wondering if we could add Sophie to our trip. She's at my house and has decided she can go after all if it's not too late."

"I'm almost sure we can add one person. When I talked with the travel agent last week, I told her we may need another ticket, and she said she would hold one more—just in case. Tell Sophie to call me tonight. I'll know for sure by then."

When I tell Sophie, her face lights up. We talk a few more minutes. I want to ask her how things are at home, but I'm afraid I'll remind her of other troubles in her life.

"By the way," she says when she gets up to leave, "Mom says to thank you for what you've done to help me. I told her all about you trying to get me to stop going over to the coach's house. She was really impressed. My mom said, 'I thought you said she was really shy. That sounds very bold to me.' She also said that you must be a very good friend."

"Tell your mom I'm trying to get over being so timid."

When Sophie leaves, I feel a little better. Maybe I missed an opportunity to stop things last spring, but I had no evidence that Coach Callahan had done anything wrong, so I might have made things worse. I am still sitting on the couch thinking back over the conversation Sophie and I had when Mom gets home.

"I thought I met Sophie as I came home. Has she been over here?"

"Yes, she just left, so I guess you did meet her."

"Is she okay?"

"I think so. She wants me to go with her to see Ms. Willoughby tomorrow morning, and she also wants to go with us on our senior trip. You know we asked her to go, but she never told me she could, so I thought she didn't want to."

"But now she does?"

"Yes, and I called Ms. Lucas, and she thinks she can get Sophie included." I tell Mom the whole story.

The next morning Sophie seems confident and ready to talk to Ms. Willoughby. "I'm glad you came with her, Alice," Ms. Willoughby says. "I was going to call you in later today anyway. The main thing I need to tell both of you is that the investigator will be ready to interview you in a few days. I'm not sure which day, but it will probably be after school on Thursday or Friday. Will that be a problem for either of you?" We look at our schedules and decide that it is not.

"Will we have to go in alone, at different times?" asks Sophie.

"I don't know. That is one reason I wanted to talk to you. Are you ready to tell them the whole story? They may get rather specific and want details that may be difficult for you to reveal. I think they will use a female detective, though, and they said that I can be in the room if it will help. Do you want me to go with you? They also said that a family member can be with you if you'd rather have your mother there instead of school personnel."

"I'd want someone there I think," Sophie said in a very low voice. It's the first time I've ever seen Sophie so withdrawn and quiet.

"Okay," says Ms. Willoughby. "I'll plan my schedule so that I can go with you if you need me. Talk to your mother and think about what you want to do. If you decide that your mother should go, just let me know. Maybe you can tell me when I give you the exact time that the police want to talk to you."

"Will they come here? I'd be mortified to have students see me being taken into the office or something." Sophie is fidgeting in a way that makes me think she is getting very upset at all this talk about talking to the police. I would be too.

"No, I think they'll want you to go down to the police station to give your deposition."

"Are you saying that I'll have to tell them everything?" asked Sophie.

"You have been taken advantage of by a school employee," says Ms. Willoughby. "That's a crime. The more honest you are, the better picture they will have of what he really did. It's important that they know in specific terms what he has done so they will know what charges can be filed. I think you should be as honest with them as you can."

"Okay," Sophie slumps in her chair.

"I know this is very difficult for you, and I want to help you in every way that I can. You know that, don't you?" Sophie nods.

"Now let's talk about your interview, Alice. The same thing applies to you. You should try to be as honest as you can with the investigators, not making accusations, but just giving them any facts will help them get a picture of what went on."

"I will," I promise.

"Another thing…," says Ms. Willoughby, "they want the names of some of the other students who went to the coach's house on a regular basis and who might have noticed his behavior, especially any girls who might have also been abused by him."

Sophie and I look at each other, and then we help compile a list of a few who went over there often. I also tell her about Todd saying that most of the students had quit going after Mrs. Callahan left, but he did not say exactly why. Sophie doesn't seem to know why either, but she verifies that they did stop going soon after the coach's wife left him.

"Have they talked to Mrs. Callahan?" asks Sophie, looking at Ms. Willoughby. "I assume they have by now, but I have not asked."

"I wish they would just finish the investigation. I'm ready for this to be over," says Sophie as we leave Ms. Willoughby's office.

I nod. "Me too." I decide to ask her something I've been wondering about. "What happened about getting a scholarship to the college in Ohio?"

"Nothing. I have applied to Kennesaw State University. I think I'll be accepted, but I haven't actually heard yet. That way I can be home more. I'll probably commute, provided I can work out a good schedule. Mom and Joline really need me now."

"That is good. I'm glad you're not going off to Ohio." I smile.

CHAPTER 28

I'm walking down the hall at school with Grace and Juan, and we're talking about our upcoming graduation trip to Cancun. I see three boys slouching against the wall by the chemistry lab. They're looking toward us and the tallest one nudges the one in the middle, smirking. As we approach, I hear him say, "There she is. Looks like she likes Mexicans, too." The other two mumble something incomprehensible to each other as they continue to look at us.

Beside me I hear Grace tell Juan, "I'm glad you'll be going to Cancun so you can interpret for us," but I'm distracted by the guys near the chemistry lab. My heart is racing now, and fear creeps into my chest as I see one of the guys edge over toward Juan and Grace. The tall one steps in front of Grace and gives Juan's wheelchair a little push forward toward the water fountain. Trying to stop the chair, Juan drops two books he is holding.

"Is that your boyfriend, Grace?" he asks, pointing toward the wheelchair.

"He's my friend, yes," she replies. I can see her swallow hard, and her face turns a little white, but she walks on quickly and gets to Juan just as he retrieves the books.

Juan turns and faces the guy. "Hey, what's your problem, man?" he states in a calm voice.

"Can't you find someone with two arms and two legs to fight? Or are you intimidated by those kinds of people?" He looks the guy straight in the eye without flinching, waiting for a response.

The guy's face gets red and he starts back toward his buddies, then turns toward Juan and says, "You'd better watch your back when you're not surrounded by your friends. And you," he says, pointing at me, "better quit accusing people of things if you know what's good for you."

Joining him, another one of the guys says, "Yeah, we don't need so many Mexicans around here anyway. When y'all go to Cancun, maybe you should just stay down there."

They stare at me for a moment, and I fear they can see the color draining from my face and the palpitations in my chest. After a few seconds, they move on down the hall, keeping that permanent smirk on their faces. It bothers me that they obviously know I have reported Coach Callahan, but I'm more concerned that they said these things about Juan. I've always thought that most of my classmates treat everyone the same. I've seen these guys before, but I don't know any of their names.

I look over at Juan, and he is just calmly talking to Grace as if nothing has happened. When he sees my face, he stops talking and says, "Hey Alice, we better get on down to class. You know they can't read Macbeth without us!" He grins that mischievous grin and heads on down the hall toward the English wing. Grace and I follow dutifully.

CHAPTER 29

The closer it gets to the end of the school year, the worse is my fear that my best friend will not achieve his goal of walking across the stage at graduation on May 26, much less go on a trip to Cancun. Since the plans were all made to go on the senior trip, Juan has started showing more signs of being sick. He won't admit it, of course, but I can tell. More and more, he relies on "Betty," and although he still goes with the gang most everywhere we go, he does not insist on doing everything by himself.

Since prom, Grace goes with Juan almost everywhere. When I see her with him, she keeps a cheerful face. But when I see her at school, she expresses her deep concern that he is getting worse. Isabella says that her mother's friends are all telling her she should not try to take Juan to Mexico. It's too risky, they say. But of course, Juan would be devastated, and Ms. Lucas says it wouldn't be fair to him to cancel at the last minute. I don't know what Ms. Willoughby thinks. We are supposed to leave about a week after graduation. Maybe he'll be better by then. I hope so.

Graduation is this Friday. On Wednesday, Grace calls me in a panic. "Juan is so sick. I don't see how he can come to graduation practice tomorrow or to the graduation ceremony. He has seemed to give up. He says he just can't do it." She sounds as if she is about in tears.

"Let me think. I'll call Ms. Lucas. Maybe she can help."

When I call Ms. Lucas, she says that a friend has suggested CBD oil might help Juan. I don't know if it actually is healing or just helps the symptoms. She says she will call her friend and see what she can find out. I call Grace back, and she seems a little bit relieved.

Later that evening, Ms. Lucas calls me to say that she has gotten some of the oil and will take it to Juan. When she gets to Juan's house, Grace and I are there to greet her.

"I don't think I should take that stuff," Juan says. "My hospice nurse said it wouldn't help." He is lying on the bed with his eyes closed.

"What you're doing now is not helping," notes Ms. Lucas.

"I'm not sure that stuff is even legal," Juan points out.

"Right now, I'm just trying to help you walk across the stage on Friday."

"Okay, I'll take it then," he says, sitting up and pulling up a pillow behind his head. We all leave after he takes his first dose of the oil. Before Ms. Lucas gets in her car, she turns to Grace and me.

"I hope it doesn't make him worse," she says. "I would feel awful if it did."

Grace and I both tell her we don't think it will hurt him. Of course, we don't know. I'm just glad she was willing to try to do something.

I get up on Thursday morning, put on some jeans and a sweatshirt, and stand looking in the pantry. Do I want cereal or oatmeal? On the kitchen counter, my phone buzzes. I go to look at it and see that it is a text from Juan. "I'm going to IHOP to eat breakfast. Want to come? Grace and Bert are on their way."

I text back, "Be there in 15 minutes." I can't believe it! He sounds like a new person. I guess Ms. Lucas's medicine is a miracle.

When I arrive, Bert is helping him out of his car. I ask him how he feels this morning.

"I feel great. Best I've felt in weeks." I want to mention to him that it's probably the CBD oil Ms. Lucas gave him, but I don't. I do text and tell her, however.

Both Grace and I are grateful that he is able to be at graduation practice, and we work out a plan so that he can walk across the stage tomorrow, wearing his prosthesis that he seldom wears. He can walk with it, but he says it's very painful, so he doesn't like to wear it.

Suddenly, it's 6 o'clock on Friday evening, and we're lining up for graduation. I see Grace, Bert, Juan, and Todd up ahead of me. I swallow hard and say a little prayer that Juan will walk without too much pain. Since Garcia and Gurley are close together alphabetically, the plan is for Todd to push Juan's wheelchair up the ramp and when Grace gets her diploma, she will come back to where they are standing and help Juan get up. She will walk across the stage with him just in case he needs someone to lean on. Bert, who will already have his diploma, will bring the wheelchair to the other side of the stage so Juan can sit back down after receiving his diploma.

I have all this in my mind as we begin to march in. When the program begins, some people from the school board are there, and one of them welcomes parents and guests. I looked for family members there to support Juan, but I don't see them. I hope his mother and brothers are here. I'm sure his godparents are, because Juan said they are coming. I see Sophie's mother and Joline, but not her dad.

The superintendent of schools comes to the platform, congratulates the seniors, and welcomes the parents and friends. After two or three other "dignitaries" make some brief comments, they call the salutatorian, Mandy, to give her speech. It's short, but she does a good job. She thanks all the students and adults who have helped her throughout high school. She doesn't go into detail about her troubles, but just mentions that she would not have been able to achieve what she has without the help of so many friends, teachers, and her family. (I've heard that her uncle is serving a long-term prison sentence because of his crimes, so hopefully the problems he caused in her life are over.) When Mandy finishes her speech, she receives a loud round of applause.

Th superintendent then calls Isabella to the lectern to give the valedictorian's speech. She talks some about her goal of being a medical scientist, and also brings in a little about how Juan has been such an inspiration to her. She also talks about how he has made the whole senior class better because of his positive attitude.

Then it is time for us to receive our diplomas. Of course, they are not really giving us our actual diplomas—just the folders. We have to come back Monday to get them. I am glad to be far enough behind Juan so that I can see him walk across the stage. He has Grace by his side, just in case he needs some help. The audience goes wild when he receives his diploma. It takes a few moments for things to settle down, and then the rest of the students file by quickly and silently. After all the students have received their folders, someone says we have fulfilled the requirements for graduation. We then change the tassels on our caps to the other side and begin to file out.

I guess most people remember their high school graduation because it means they are finishing one phase of life and beginning another. I will remember it mostly because it means that Juan has achieved a difficult goal. Right now, that is the only thing that matters. It's a day he's been hoping for throughout high school. Several times he's told me that he doubted he'd make it. I always told him I thought he would, but sometimes I only pretended. Now we will celebrate with him in achieving that goal. Maybe he will set another goal. No matter what else happens, he walked across that stage!

Grace has invited about 20 of us to a graduation party at her house. She has a pool and we can bring our swim suits if we want. It's still a little cool outside, but the pool is open. As soon as we all get there, Juan announces that he wants to go swimming. He loves the water. Grace and most of his other friends question the wisdom of his decision, but there is no stopping him. He says he has a change of clothes, and he WILL go swimming! Before we can say much about it, he jumps in the pool—clothes and all—and floats along the pool, paddling with his one arm. Not to be outdone, several others jump in after him, but since it is actually too cold to be comfortable, soon they all come shivering out and wrap up in their towels. I didn't even get in. I knew I wouldn't like it, because I hate to swim in cold water. After each person gets dressed in the pool house restroom, we go inside and have snacks, including a huge cake with "Congratulations Graduates" written across the chocolate icing in our school colors of green and white.

Juan rode to the party with Grace, but Ms. Lucas and Isabella are taking him home. I see him say something to Grace, and not long after that, Ms. Lucas says they need to leave. I wonder if Juan isn't feeling well. When they leave, I ask Grace if she thinks he will be able to go to Cancun. She sighs and says, "I hope so." I can see the worry in her eyes, but she doesn't say more.

With all the excitement of graduation and the worry over Juan's health, I haven't thought too much about the investigation into Coach Callahan. I haven't talked to Sophie much since our interviews at the police department, and I haven't heard Todd or Juan say anything about the police contacting them. I think we are all afraid to say anything, because we don't know who knows about it or what they think about it. I have asked Mom if she's heard anything, but she hasn't. I hope we learn something before we go on our senior trip. I think Sophie will feel better if we do.

The next week, Ms. Lucas comes over and talks to Mom about the CBD oil she has been giving Juan. "He doesn't want to take it with him to Cancun," she says. She looks at Mom and shrugs.

"He seems to be doing a little better since he's been taking it," Mom comments.

"Exactly. I'm afraid if he doesn't take it, he'll be right back where he was just before graduation, so I've told him I'll have it with me. Nobody thinks I should take him on that trip, but he'd be so disappointed if we cancel."

"You'll have to do what you think best. I don't know what to advise. What do Grace and her mother think?"

"They're kind of leaving it up to me, but I think they would hate to cancel."

"You have done so much for Juan," I tell her. "If you are willing to risk taking him, I think you should make the decision."

Ms. Lucas gives me a hug. "Thank you, Alice. I needed that. Several of my friends are being critical that I'm even still considering taking him, but he wants to go so badly." I can tell she is hurt by the attitude of her friends.

We have bought extra insurance for the trip because Juan's Medicaid will not work outside the country. That is one reason so many people think it's unwise for him to go.

"Like Alice said, I think it's your decision," says Mom.

Ms. Lucas looks down. "Sometimes I think we just have to trust God. If it were Isabella, I'd take her—and I'd give her the CBD oil. Juan is just like my own child. I couldn't love him more if he were my son." Tears begin to pour out of her eyes.

Mom pats her on the shoulder. "Juan is lucky to have a 'mom' like you."

Chapter 30

Since Juan was so sick just a few days before graduation, I am worried every day that he might not be able to make our trip to Cancun. I text him regularly to ask how he's feeling. The night before our trip when I text him, I think he suspects I am afraid he is not well enough to go—which is partially true. He sends a message back: "Stop texting me! Of course, I'm okay. I'm going on a big trip in the morning, so I'm packing." He puts a smiling emoji next to the words to let me know he's not mad.

At 6 o'clock the next morning, Mom drives us to the school to meet the others going on the trip. I have tried to pack light, but I can still barely pick up my suitcase. Juan is the last to arrive. His godmother drove him here on her way to work.

"Whose idea was it to leave so early?" gripes Juan.

"Delta," answers Ms. Lucas, laughing as she tries to fit all the luggage, the wheelchair, and other stuff into our vehicle. Ms. Willoughby managed to borrow a school system van, and Mom is driving us to the airport. Then she'll use it again to pick us up when we return from the trip.

Our ride to Atlanta early in the morning on Saturday is smooth sailing with little traffic. I am relieved to see that Juan seems to be feeling fine and in high spirits. Ms. Lucas told us last night that, despite Juan's objections, she has brought the CBD oil along and he has agreed to take it during our trip.

"Can you believe we are actually high school graduates?" asks Grace as we approach the airport. We all shake our heads.

"Another question," says Juan. "Do you know any other guy who is going on a senior trip with four girls?" We all burst out laughing.

"Just remember," cautions Ms. Lucas, "You've also got two chaperones along with you. So don't try anything."

When Mom drops us off with all our stuff, we look like a bunch of geeks I guess, but we are laughing and having fun. Of course, as we learned when we traveled to California, traveling with Juan is a bit of a challenge, but he's a trooper. It takes TSA at least 30 minutes to get him checked through security, since he can't go through the x-ray machine. Eventually, though, we are on our way to the gate where we are able to eat breakfast and wait to board our plane.

Upon boarding the plane, Juan is prepared to reject the little "aisle chair" like the one given him on our trip to California—he hated it—but the flight attendants don't even offer him one. He just hops to his seat as he would in other situations. He and Grace sit together. Isabella, Ms. Lucas, and Ms. Willoughby are grouped in three middle seats. And Sophie and I are seated together.

When we arrive in Cancun, we quickly realize how lucky we are to have Juan with us. I hadn't really thought that much about the fact that we might have problems understanding so many things. Since Juan was born in the U.S. and I see him mostly with other people speaking English, I have not heard him speak Spanish that much. As soon as we get off the plane, though, I'm having trouble understanding the signs and conversations around me. Then we have to exchange our money for a different kind of currency. Fortunately, Juan is very familiar with everything. From then on, we all stick close to him.

"Do you now see how difficult it is for some of my friends who haven't been in the U.S. very long?" Juan asks. "There are so many things they have trouble with."

"I always try to be helpful to those students when they come, but I'm getting an education now on how difficult it must be. They're fortunate to have someone like you for a friend, Juan," says Ms. Willoughby.

"We're all fortunate to have Juan for a friend, aren't we?" concurs Ms. Lucas.

"Yeah, if I ran off and left all of you here, you'd be doomed." Juan teases.

"I don't think that will happen though," says Isabella, pushing his wheelchair.

"Unless he gets a motorized wheelchair," adds Sophie.

"Or I could go with him, and leave all of you behind," says Grace, laughing.

"I guess we'll just all hang out together, and I'll interpret for you—since you all obviously need me so much," Juan says.

Our hotel is close to the beach, and we spend most of our time either at the pool or the ocean. Juan loves the beach. We push him in the wheelchair, and then carry him over to an umbrella, where he sits in a chair and listens to some music he brought along. Sometimes he takes a nap for a while. The rest of us sit with him part of the time, and at other times we go down to the water. When we don't go down to the beach, Juan loves to swim and float in the pool. In the evening we go out to eat. Juan talks to the hotel manager and finds out which restaurants are the best. Then he helps us get a cab and figure out our money.

We go to restaurants that have authentic Mexican food, which Juan loves. At one of the restaurants, I order the same food as Juan does. But when I taste it, I almost gag. "What is this? It's gross." Juan just laughs at me.

One day we see this ad for a snorkeling park located about an hour from our hotel. Juan reads the details for us and decides he wants to go.

"I think it's not too far from where my mother is from, and I want to see where it is."

"Is it wheelchair accessible?" asks Ms. Lucas.

"Yes. It says so right here," he answers, pointing to some of the text.

"So, are we going to where your mother grew up?" questions Sophie. "Wow! That is so exciting!"

"No, I didn't say that. I just said it might be the general area of where she came from. She's hardly ever talked about it."

"Does she know we are in Mexico?" asks Isabella.

"Yeah, I told her, but she didn't say much. I've heard her say she's been to Cancun, and one time she said something about a place that might have been this place. I don't know really. I'd just like to go see what it's like."

"Then let's do it," urges Ms. Lucas. "It'll be fun for all of us."

We take a bus to the snorkeling site. It is a natural area, where you also can go tubing and on a zip line. It turns out that it is not accessible by wheelchair, however. The first thing Juan wants to do is get on the zip line. When he realizes that he cannot get up there, he is very frustrated and ready to go back to the hotel.

"We can help you," says Grace. We all agree.

"But you all are just a bunch of girls," he argues.

"Girls can do anything we want," states Sophie. "Don't tell us we can't."

Finally, we carry Juan up to the zip line and help him get on it, laughing all the way. It's not an easy task, but we're all so excited that he is getting to do this. He is so happy. You would never know he is sick. When he is on the zipline, we all cry because he's doing something he really wants to do.

When it comes to the snorkeling, Juan gets even more frustrated because he can't wear his glasses with the mask. And, he can't see worth anything without them. But Grace encourages him to do it anyway.

"You'll know how it feels to go snorkeling, even if you can't see much. You may be surprised at how much you can actually see."

"Yeah, surely there are other people who go snorkeling who have trouble seeing," adds Isabella.

As we get back on the bus, I think what a good day it has been, one I—and everyone else—will always remember. As I am with all our activities with Juan lately, I am both happy and sad—happy because he is so much fun to have around, sad because I am afraid it won't last. He achieved his goal of walking across the stage and getting his high school diploma, but that's not enough for any of us. Juan just says he is living every day to the fullest. He refuses to get caught up in worry about what will happen next. He even plans to enroll in the local community college this fall.

This evening we go back to the restaurant that Juan says is the best one. "The guy at the hotel says he goes there two or three times a week. I want to eat there again tonight. You all want to go back there, too. Right?"

"Of course," we all say obediently and grin.

"So, it's settled then."

Isabella and I have been like sisters to Juan for a long time, and to some extent Sophie has too. Although Sophie hasn't been with us quite as much, she is so outgoing that she bonds with people quickly. Since joining the debate team in 10th grade, she has spent a lot of time with Juan. And then there's Grace.

After returning to the hotel, we girls just sit on our beds and talk.

"What's it like to have Juan as a boyfriend?" Sophie is the one who can always get right to the point of things. "And how did you two decide you liked each other enough to date?"

Isabella and I are shocked at Sophie's directness, but Grace is not. "Grace" is a perfect name for her.

"Well," she begins, "it was a gradual realization. At the beginning, we just became friends. But eventually I think we both realized that we could see a future together."

She stops and looks at our faces. "Now, I know what you're thinking. We didn't even know each other well until after Juan had been told by the doctors that he had only three to six months to live. We both know that and have talked about it. But I'm just telling you about our realization. When you think about it, no one knows how long they'll live. All we know is how we think and feel about each other. So, we just live one day at a time. Right now, I want to become a nurse, and Juan wants to work toward college graduation. We may or may not be able to do what we want to, but we both imagine that whatever we do, we'd like to do it together for as long as we can."

"And you both have a strong faith. I'm sure that helps," says Isabella.

"That's one thing that attracted me to Juan," says Grace. "I actually got to know him when he started coming to our youth group at church. I was so impressed with how positive and supportive he was."

"You didn't know him before?" I ask.

"I had seen him around school in his wheelchair, but I hadn't talked to him much. One night in youth group, one of the 9th graders got upset about something. I don't remember what it was. Probably an upper classman had made a snide remark about freshmen. That happens sometimes, even at church."

"What did you do?" asks Isabella.

"I didn't do anything, but I noticed Juan looking over at him. When the meeting was over, Juan wheeled himself over to the 9th grader and asked the boy if he would help him get out to the car. As I was leaving, I saw the boy standing next to Juan's car. I heard enough of their conversation to realize that Juan was apologizing to him for whatever had upset him. Juan hadn't upset him, of course. Most of the youth depend on Juan a lot for encouragement."

"Do you ever feel the weight of knowing you'll have to take care of Juan all the time?" asks Sophie. "I know you love him, and he's a great person, but it just seems like it would be hard to deal with all the time."

Grace sighs. "No, I don't see it that way. First of all, we both have our problems. You may not know this, but I have had diabetes since I was in preschool. I have to be very careful what I eat, and I have to give myself insulin injections every day."

Sophie, Isabella, and I are all shocked. "No," says Sophie. "I did not know."

"So, you see," said Grace, "there are times when I have to lean on Juan when I have a bad day. Our health challenges are different, but we both have them."

"How did you learn to give yourself shots?" asks Isabella. "I would have a hard time with that."

"When I was in elementary school, I went to these summer camps where they teach kids how to control their diabetes. It was fun to be with other children who had the same problems, and I really don't remember that it was that hard to learn about the injections."

All too quickly, our days in Cancun are over and it is time to go home. Although none of us say so, we're sad to see this day come. The van taking us from the hotel to the airport is quiet as we each reflect on our last few days. I realize how fortunate we are to have had this time together. On the plane most of us take a nap, since we had to awake early to leave.

When we arrive at the Atlanta airport, Mom is there waving at us. I run toward her and give her a hug.

"Well, how was Cancun?" she asks.

We all assure her that we had a great time. Then she points toward the parking area, and we all head that way. Dragging our luggage behind us, we take turns helping Juan with his.

When we arrive back in Closeville, before we get off the van, Juan shouts out, "Hey, I have something to say!"

We sit quietly for a moment, and Mom gives Juan the microphone at the front of the van. "Here, use this."

"I just want to thank you, Ms. Lucas and Ms. Willoughby, for making this trip possible. And I… (I think he is going to break down and cry, but he regains his composure.) I also want to thank Grace, Alice, Sophie, and Isabella for helping to make this a fun trip. You will never know how much it means to me." He stops, looks around and grins. "Of course, I know that none of you could have found your way around without me there to speak the language."

We all begin to cheer loudly and agree with Juan. We look out the window and family members and friends waiting to pick us up, including Rosa who is there to pick up Juan. We did it! We made Juan's trip to Cancun a reality.

CHAPTER 31

The first thing I ask Mom when we get back in our car alone is whether she has heard about the results of the police investigation into the Callahan case.

"We heard two days ago," she tells me. "He's in jail and probably will be until the trial, but they haven't set a date for it yet."

"Will I have to testify?" I ask.

"I don't know. Your deposition might be enough, but I would not rule out the possibility that they'll ask some of the students to testify."

"Will Sophie have to testify?"

"Again, I'm not sure."

"I hope we won't. I hate that kind of thing. I know Sophie is already so embarrassed. She'll hate it if she has to get up there and be asked questions while people who know her are looking on."

Sophie and I receive our subpoenas the same day. She calls me all upset at first, but after I tell her that I have to go to court, she seems to calm down a bit.

It turns out both Todd and Juan were able to corroborate Sophie's testimony on several issues. At the time they heard a conversation or two about the scholarship deal, they didn't really understand what was at stake, but it made sense to the investigators because of what Sophie had told them in her deposition. A trial date is now set.

For the rest of the summer after our Cancun trip, Juan continues to hang out with all of us. Grace is with him almost all the time. Isabella, Sophie, and I see them almost every day. We reminisce about our trip and talk about our plans for college. Grace and Juan will both be at the local community college, and Grace will enter nursing school after completing her core requirements. Sophie will commute to Kennesaw, and Isabella and I will leave the first week in September.

We are all careful not to discuss Juan's prognosis. We can see that he will probably not live long enough to finish college. Nevertheless, we hold out hope that by some miracle of medicine or God, or both, we will not lose Juan. He has always maintained that he wants to live life to its fullest for as long as it lasts, so he never wants us to be morbid. As time goes on, however, his lungs seem to be losing power, and it's beginning to show more and more. I dread the day I have to leave Closeville and go away to college. I imagine that one day I'll get a call saying that my best friend is gone. Each time we part during the summer, I get a lump in my throat. But each time, I make myself put those thoughts aside and say, "See you tomorrow," and mean it.

Coach Callahan's trial begins on a Monday and is expected to be finished by the end of the week. Sophie testifies that day, but the rest of us are not allowed in the courtroom. I learn from Ms. Willoughby that Sophie was a very credible witness and did a good job of responding to the cross-examiner's questions. On the second day Juan, Todd, and I are called to testify, but we are only in the courtroom during our own questioning. Both my parents come with me.

I am escorted into the courtroom alone. I look around the room, noticing that there are several parents of students sitting in the audience, staring at me as if I am the criminal. I have heard that several of them are very angry about the charges brought against the coach. I see one of those girls who approached me in the hall that day and harassed me. My heart is pounding. I feel small and scared. I see Coach Callahan seated at the defense table and his attorneys beside him. I tell myself I am not afraid, that I am not the one on trial. I calm down a little when I see the prosecuting attorney approach the witness stand.

Most of the questions the prosecutor asks me center around my observations on the night I went to the Callahan's house and on my later conversations with Sophie. When he finishes, the defense attorney starts to cross-examine me. He keeps saying, "And did you hear or see Mr. Callahan do anything to Sophie that night?"

Of course, I have to say, "No."

"Did you see Mr. Callahan touch your friend in an inappropriate manner?"

"No."

"Did you hear him say anything to her that was inappropriate?"

"No."

"So, you don't really know whether he did anything wrong, or if your friend was just lying, do you?"

"No, but…"

"That's all, your honor."

I go home feeling that I probably didn't help Sophie's case. I didn't really know anything for sure. I apologize to Sophie, but she says I don't need to. All anyone expects is for us to tell the truth, and I did. We decide that we don't want to attend the court proceedings tomorrow morning, but Sophie's mother is going.

On Wednesday morning, Sophie comes over to my house and we listen to music and talk about college and anything besides the trial. The coach's ex-wife is called to testify. Sophie's mother calls afterward to say that she gave some very damaging testimony. It seems that she revealed some things she observed involving Sophie and one other girl. Apparently, the other girl, who was called to testify, had graduated last year. I don't recognize her name, and don't know when she testified. Just before noon, the prosecution rests its case. Sophie and I decide that we want to hear the testimonies of the defense witnesses.

After the lunch break, we are in the courtroom when the attorneys approach the bench to confer with the judge. We can't hear their conversation. The defense attorney then begins the direct examination of witnesses. The first one is the athletic director for Closeville High School. The attorney tries to establish the fact that the director has had no previous complaints about the coach, and that he came here with a good recommendation. Upon cross-examination, though, the athletic director admits that he didn't know much about Callahan before he came here.

The defense attorney only has time for one more witness, and she is the parent of one of the girls on the basketball team. During the direct examination, the woman is first asked what she thinks of Coach Callahan, and she describes him in glowing terms. Then she is led to imply that Sophie might be considered a "flirt" by some of the students. I am appalled that the attorney would do that. I watch Sophie, but she sits stoically in her seat. When we leave, she tells me that the prosecutor had warned her that they would try to make her look like it was her fault.

On Thursday morning, the defense continues to call witnesses. The first one is a psychiatrist who testifies that Callahan was abused as a child. During cross-examination the psychiatrist admits that, according to the law, the fact that he had been abused would not excuse him for abusing a student.

The second witness is a longtime friend of Callahan's, who says that the coach has never been in trouble with the law or accused of any crime.

"But you're not saying that you know anything about his actions in regard to this case, are you?" asks the prosecutor during cross-examination.

"No," admits the witness.

When the defense rests its case, the attorney makes his closing statements. The prosecutor then gives his final arguments. The judge instructs the jury to get organized for their work and then to take a lunch break before beginning deliberations this afternoon.

Not knowing how long they will be, Sophie and I decide to go to lunch and then go home and return later in the afternoon.

Mom and Sophie's mom go back over to the courthouse before we do.

About 2:45, Sophie gets a text from her mother. "They may be ready to come back with a verdict soon."

"That's quick," Sophie says. "Do you think that's good or bad?"

"I don't know. But it means they didn't have much disagreement."

We hurry back to the courthouse and wait. About 3:30, the jury comes back in. Sophie is holding on to my arm as they file in. The foreman of the jury reads the verdict: guilty on several counts. And when the judge polls the jury, they are unanimous in their decision. Sophie's tears start to fall as the reality sinks in for her. I put my arm around her on one side, and her mother holds her on the other. She doesn't say anything, but I feel the relief in her body as we walk out. It's been a long year, but it's time to begin anew.

The court is dismissed and a tentative date is set for the sentencing. Mom and I leave, but Sophie and her mother stay to talk to the judge and the attorneys. Before we leave, I tell Sophie to text or call me when she gets home. Mom tells me that the sentencing will be after I leave for college.

"Do you feel sorry for Coach Callahan?" I ask.

"I'm sorry for whatever happened to him as a child," she says. "But as an adult, I think he'll have to be accountable for his actions."

I am exhausted. I think I've been tense the whole week. I don't know how Sophie has gone through all the questioning, prying eyes, and sneering looks. I didn't know people could be so ugly.

When Sophie calls me, she informs me that she and her mother have declined to attend the sentencing.

"I don't think our being there will change the outcome. I want him to be held accountable, but I don't think I can go through anymore. From what the prosecutor said, it will be a matter of using the guidelines, and then reducing it a few years if there are some extenuating circumstances that might warrant it."

"I don't blame you. Besides, by the time of the sentencing, you'll probably be at Kennesaw State every day and busy with assignments."

"That's what we decided. I just want to get on with my life."

I guess that's what we all want—to get on with our lives. Although I don't want to be separated from my friends, I am being pulled forward to a new life. Mom and I begin shopping for what I'll need for my dorm room and for the extra clothes I may need.

CHAPTER 32

By the time Isabella and I are ready to leave for college, Juan is noticeably worse. Grace is staying with him most days, and when his godparents have to be gone, he often goes to her house and stays a few days. She is getting a lot of practice being a nurse. I don't know if I could do what she does or not. I have started going to Grace's church most weeks.

One Wednesday night as I'm leaving the parking lot after our college Bible study, the pastor stops me and ask, "Could I talk to you a minute?"

"Of course." I have seldom talked to him except in a group, so I'm not sure what to say.

"Some of the people here are worried about Grace," he begins.

"Yes? What exactly are they worried about?"

"I think they are afraid she will get so involved with caring for Juan that she won't go to college and nursing school as she has planned."

"Are her parents concerned?" I ask.

"I haven't heard anything from them," he admits.

"They are involved in caring for Juan too."

"I'm not sure everyone knows that. That makes a difference."

"I think Grace is going to do what she can for Juan, but I think she'll go to nursing school eventually."

"Thank you, Alice. You have made me feel better about Grace. I don't know Grace and her family and Juan very well, so I want to understand when I talk to those who are concerned."

Juan, Grace, and I spend a lot of time together all summer. When the local schools start back, we continue to go everywhere together. We watch the teams practice and attend the first football game. At times Juan seems a little better. He and Grace enroll in the community college. She usually drives him to school or waits and helps him out of his car when he gets there. One of his friends is making him a contraption that is supposed to allow him to get out of his car without help. He is all excited about it, but by the time it is finished, Juan is too weak to use it.

I have mixed feelings about going to Auburn now. I have talked to my roommates. There are four of us in a suite. Each of us has our own small bedroom, and there are two baths. One of the girls lives only about an hour from Auburn. She says that she considered commuting, but her mother wants her to live on campus.

When I think of all this, I am truly excited about college. On the other hand, I am worried about Juan. Also, I have spent more time with Sophie the last few weeks and realize how much she has been hurt by all that has happened to her. She seems to really need my friendship right now.

The day before I leave home is a busy one. By late afternoon, I'm wondering how in the world I'll be able to get everything packed. Sophie comes over after lunch and we sit on my bed quietly amid all the boxes of clothes, bed linens, and other stuff I've packed. She looks over at the bright posters I've made to put on the walls of my dorm room.

"So, you're leaving tomorrow?"

"Yes, tomorrow around noon."

"Are you scared?"

"Not really… Well, a little. But I'm excited too."

"I can't believe this is you, and I'm the one staying in town. You remember that time I questioned whether you'd be able to defend a friend like me or Todd? That was only a little more than a year ago. It seems like a lifetime, though."

I nod. "A lot has happened since then."

"It seems as though we've almost changed roles, doesn't it? Here I am, weak and almost afraid to go out of the house, and you … you stood up in the courtroom and told the truth with such force that no one could contradict you."

I look at her. "Don't be hard on yourself, Sophie. You've been through a lot. You'll get back to yourself again. It'll just take some time."

"I hope so. But I'm proud of you. It seems like your strength was just waiting inside you for when it was needed. I watched you in that courtroom. You almost seemed like a different person."

"I am a different person, Sophie. I guess it all began that day you challenged me to overcome my fears. I've thought about that several times. I remember you asking me, 'What if a friend needed you to stand up for her? Could you do it?' At the time I knew I couldn't, but I promised myself to push harder. Then when I realized you were in trouble, I just had to stand up when it counted."

When it is time for Sophie to leave, we hug each other and promise to keep in touch. We both have tears in our eyes when she goes out the door.

The day is finally here. I'm heading to Auburn University! I'm scared, but I think I can do it. Since I have more "stuff" for my dorm room than I can get in my Honda, Mom and Dad follow in her SUV. When we arrive, there are student volunteers to help freshmen move in. They are friendly and welcoming. In a very short time, my belongings are all in my room in no particular order. My roommates and I all arrive within an hour of one another. We quickly decide which bedrooms we will use—even though they're all alike. At first all the parents are introducing themselves, and my roommates and I are getting to know each other. It is chaos! Eventually things begin to calm down, and Mom and Dad go outside with some of the other parents.

It's late in the afternoon, and Mom comes inside for a moment. "I guess it's time we head back to Closeville. It's an hour later there than it is here."

"I know." For a moment, my heart speeds up a bit. Are they really leaving me here by myself? Do I have what I need to actually live here? Will my roommates like me? What have I forgot to bring?

"Alice?" Mom is saying. "Are you okay?"

"Oh, yes. I'm sorry." I straighten up a little. "I was just wondering if I've forgotten anything important at home."

"Well, if you have, you can probably find it here in Auburn. There's a Walmart just down the road," Dad says, laughing. He gives me a hug. "Come on, Mom, she'll be fine here."

As they drive off, part of me is crying out, "Are you really leaving me here to live with these strangers?"

I don't have much time to be sad or homesick the rest of the week. Every minute is planned. There are orientation meetings and Rush activities. I had only a vague idea of what "Rush" meant before I came here, and I am trying to get to know my roommates. I think Kate is similar to me in many ways, but I like the other girls too. We all seem to get along fine.

We are all hoping to pledge one of the sororities. Rush feels like a week at camp, waking up early, going all day with a packed lunch, and being so exhausted at night that I just want to go straight to bed. I have no time to think of anything else. I am meeting so many people and trying to see if I fit in anywhere.

My roommates and I sit around and talk about which sororities we like and where we may fit in. As always, I find myself listening to the others talking and trying to decide what to say. Suddenly I become aware of what Kate is saying.

"I was always so shy in high school that I never would have thought I'd even participate in Rush Week, but here I am," she says, laughing.

"Really? You were shy in high school?"

"I was, and I still am, but I'm better."

"That sounds a lot like me, but you don't seem shy at all."

"You don't either." She is shaking her head at me and laughing, her blond hair falling just along her shoulders.

On bid day I am thrilled when I am accepted into Alpha Delta Pi because that was my first choice. When I first met my ADPi family, I felt a little out of place and disappointed, but during our sisterhood retreat at the lake this weekend, I'm hanging out with some girls I really like. I think they will be some of my best friends.

Even though I haven't been homesick, and I've made some good friends, living on my own has been a big adjustment. Mom is not here to remind me to pick up my clothes or do my laundry. On the other hand, I can do whatever I want with my free time. Mom is not asking me to do an errand for her. I can eat whenever and whatever I want.

Before classes start, I meet with my advisor and learn what I'll do as a participant in the exploratory program. Like Ms. Willoughby, she makes me feel comfortable about the fact that, unlike most of my friends, I haven't chosen a major yet.

Classes are very different here in college. In high school, my teachers kept up with our assignments and reminded us of upcoming deadlines. Now I have to figure it all out. All my work in my five or six classes depends totally on me. I love only going to class two or three hours a day, though. But I have to figure out how to use the rest of the day. It's another adjustment I'm trying to make.

In just a few weeks, I have settled into a comfortable routine. I feel at home here. I talk to Juan once a week. He always says he is fine and going to classes almost all the time. As time goes on, I begin to rely on Grace more to get the picture of Juan's health. It is true that he is still attending classes some, but he also is often confined to bed for two or three days at a time. She says he sometimes coughs up blood.

It seems like no time before it is time for finals at the end of my first semester. When I go home between semesters, I see Juan, Sophie, and Grace every day. Although Juan tries to fool me, I can see that he is much weaker than he was when I left for college. But he still has his sense of humor.

A week later I'm back at Auburn when I get the call I have dreaded ever since last summer. I don't recognize the number, but I recognize the voice.

"Is this Alice?" the shaky voice asks. I realize immediately that it is Rosa, Juan's godmother. The fact that she is calling can only mean one thing.

"Yes."

"Right after you left last week, Juan handed me the names and numbers of a few people I should call when he… when he… He's gone, Alice." She and I sit in silence for a few moments, miles apart but close in spirit.

"I'll be in town by tomorrow," I say.

I've had Juan in my life ever since 7th grade. Who'll tell me that I can do it? Who will say, "If I can smile, you can smile"? I will always hear his voice and see his smile. I will always see him running across the soccer field in 7th grade. I will see his face when he walks into the Ellen DeGeneres studio and sees his name on a dressing room. I will hear him calling Ms. Lucas "Mom," and yelling at her because she has told him to be careful on a rocky slope in Cancun. I will see his determination when he tells me the doctor has said he has three to six months to live, but then boasts, "He just doesn't know Juan Garcia. I will get my high school diploma!" And I will see him walking across the stage on graduation night and hear the eruption of applause and cheers from his school family, our family, rooting for all of us.

CHAPTER 33

It has been six months now since Juan "passed from this life to the next," as his pastor said at the funeral. I wonder what Juan would have thought about the service. I think he would have complained about all the attention, but secretly he would have appreciated it.

Grace gave a sweet recounting of the way she and Juan held on to their faith during the last weeks of his life. Several other people recounted the way Juan had supported them during various problems they had. Some told of his sense of humor. He could even joke about his amputations. He would say, "Ask me what my favorite restaurant is." When the responder asked him, he'd say, "IHOP!" Then he'd burst into laughter while the listener sat there and tried to decide whether he should laugh or not.

The pastor of his church had known Juan only one year before he died. He told the audience that Juan had a strong faith. "He showed us what hope looked like, sounded like, and where that hope can be found—in Christ alone." Someone remembered that Juan believed he would be whole again after death, able to run and play soccer.

In some ways I wish I had spoken too. I have lots of good memories of my friend. But I could never have stood up in front of all those people to share them, and Juan would not have expected me to. I have come a long way this past year. I'm glad I was able to report the abuse Sophie was going through and to testify in court, but speaking at Juan's funeral would have been a different matter. Juan's life was a blessing to mine, and his death is a great loss. In many ways he is the reason I've made progress and become more confident. It's just not something I could have told a huge crowd of people.

I will soon enter my sophomore year at Auburn. Todd will begin his second year at Toccoa Falls College, where he is on the basketball team and was awarded a scholarship to help with his expenses. And Sophie will begin her second year at Kennesaw. She likes it there and is able to save money by living at home. She seems happy now. It's hard to believe it has been almost a year since she had to deal with Coach Callahan's trial. He has been sentenced to 10 years in prison for his actions in regard to Sophie.

In a few weeks Bert will continue at George Washington University in Washington, D.C. When he came back for Juan's service, he said he considered transferring to the West Coast to be closer to his parents but decided to stay in Washington where he'll have better internship opportunities relating to a career as a diplomat. I'm glad that Juan had the opportunity to attend college for one semester. Grace, who is still pursuing her goal of being a nurse, said that was a bonus for him. Isabella will be back at Case Western, hoping to begin some cancer research this year.

Life goes on. Juan's life was shorter than most, but he made a tremendous impact on all who knew him. When I look back on my high school years, I am grateful for the kind of school and community I had. We all had our problems, but we all supported each other. Most of us might not be where we are today without one another. At the time, I thought I didn't contribute much, but now I realize that confronting Sophie's problem may have saved her from much more hurt. There are those who'd say dreadful things about Closeville High School because of what Coach Callahan did, but I am lucky to have been a student there. Even Coach Callahan did some good, despite the horrible mistakes he made. I think he was flawed, just as the rest of us are, and now he is paying for his mistakes. Maybe if he had had the kind of support somewhere along the way that I had, he wouldn't have made those mistakes. I don't know all the answers, but I do know this: It isn't what happens to us that makes the difference in our lives; it's how we respond to the things that happen to us.